Glad Tidings

*A Flash Fiction
Advent Calendar*

Angie Thompson

Quiet Waters Press

Lynchburg, Virginia

Copyright © 2021 by Angie Thompson

First published July 2021

All rights reserved. No portion of this book may be reproduced in any form without permission from the publisher, except as permitted by U.S. copyright law. For permissions, email: contact@quietwaterspress.com

Cover design by Angie Thompson
Photo elements by ArtistMEF, licensed through DesignBundles.net
Sheep logo adapted from original at PublicDomainPictures.net
Scripture quoted in "Star" taken from the New King James Version. ©1982 by Thomas Nelson, Inc. Used by permission. All rights reserved.
All other scripture quotations taken from the King James Version

This is a work of fiction. Names, characters, places, and incidents are the products of the author's imagination or are used fictitiously. Any resemblance to actual events, locales, or persons, living or dead, is entirely coincidental.

ISBN: 978-1-951001-19-3 (pbk)
ISBN: 978-1-951001-20-9 (ePub)

Publisher's Cataloging-in-Publication data

Names: Thompson, Angie, author.
Title: Glad tidings : a flash fiction Advent calendar / by Angie Thompson.
Description: Lynchburg, Virginia : Quiet Waters Press, 2021. | Summary: Twenty-five short works based on themes from the Christmas story.
Identifiers: ISBN 9781951001193 (softcover) | ISBN 9781951001209 (epub)
Subjects: LCSH: Christmas stories. | Short stories. | BISAC: FICTION / Christian / General.
Classification: LCC PS3620.H649 G53 2021

*For everyone who sees him or herself in one of these stories.
May you know God's love and feel His presence
this Christmas season and always.*

*Very special thanks to Katja (@oldfashionedbooklove)
and Abigail (@readreviewrejoice)
for the blog/Instagram challenge that provided
these prompts and the motivation to write them!*

*Thanks to every family member, friend, author,
and random person who inspired any part of these stories.
It would take pages to mention you all by name, but I could
never have finished this project without the inspiration
I've gleaned from all of you over the years!*

*Special thanks to all the early readers who cheered me on and
kept me going as I was working on this project and to everyone
who gave input on the various rounds of cover design!*

Table of Contents

Day 1: Taxation 1
Day 2: Lineage 3
Day 3: Bethlehem 7
Day 4: Inn 11
Day 5: Stable 15
Day 6: Child 19
Day 7: Swaddling Clothes 23
Day 8: Manger 27
Day 9: Shepherds 31
Day 10: Night 35
Day 11: Flock 39
Day 12: Glory 43
Day 13: Angels 47
Day 14: Fear Not 51
Day 15: Glad Tidings 55
Day 16: Sign 59
Day 17: Praise 63
Day 18: Wonder 67
Day 19: Star 71
Day 20: Wise Men 75
Day 21: King 79
Day 22: Ponder 83
Day 23: Jerusalem 87
Day 24: Adore 91
Day 25: Gifts 95

Day 1: Taxation

"How much?" The question that had been looming in Jane's mind all evening finally passed her lips as her husband carefully closed the slim ledger. He shook his head slowly, and her hand instinctively rose to her rounded middle. "Clare? Will it—will it cover the taxes?"

Clare drew a deep breath and let it out wearily.

"It'll cover them. Barely."

"But isn't that—what we needed? What we prayed for?" Hope lit Jane's eyes, but her husband's shoulders drooped further.

"It's the taxes and only the taxes, Janie. Nothing else until spring, unless I can pick up odd jobs or sell some firewood. No new coat for you. Nothing nice for the baby."

"Never mind my coat. I'll be staying close to home until the baby's born anyway, even if we're not snowed in. And the baby won't know any difference for a long while yet. But if we can pay the taxes, we can keep the farm. That's most important."

Clare swallowed hard and looked away. Jane carefully got to her feet and crossed over to perch on his knees.

"What is it? We've been so worried about the taxes all year, but God's provided. What more could we ask?"

"I made a promise, Janie. After last year, I promised myself— you'd never go without a Christmas again."

Glad Tidings

"Oh, Clare." Jane rested her head on his shoulder, tears of remorse stinging her eyes at the memory of the first Christmas morning they'd spent together. "I didn't need all those things I said—honest I didn't. I was tired and lonely and half sick; you know I was. And you made it up to me in a hundred ways. I wouldn't trade it now for anything. Truly I wouldn't."

"It'd be a long time before I could give you everything." Clare's voice was low and husky. "But I promised myself this year I'd give you—something. If it wasn't for the taxes..."

"If it wasn't for the taxes, we couldn't keep the farm. Don't you think I'm just as set on that as you are? A farm that's ours for another year—that's more than just a roof over our heads, Clare. I don't see how I could want anything more."

"Janie—"

"You'll read the Christmas story again, won't you? And isn't there a pine bough down by the creek that we could put in the window? With a candle in it, you know. We can spare a candle, surely. I'll even go to bed half an hour earlier every night till spring to make it up. And I dried enough berries from that last picking to make a real good pie. Mrs. Tanner gave me the recipe. Oh, we'll have Christmas, Clare! Such a Christmas as you've never seen. With everything we've got to be thankful for, I don't see how anyone can say it's not Christmas for us."

Clare's eyes were shimmering wet in the dim firelight by the time she finished, and he pulled her close as his voice cracked.

"I still don't have anything to give you, Janie."

"Don't you? Haven't you? Didn't you work your fingers near to the bone to keep this place and pay those blessed taxes? Didn't you pick me out of all the world when there were a hundred other girls who could've helped you so much more?"

"Never wanted another girl." The words were rough and choked against her hair, and Jane wrapped an arm around his shoulders as they began to shake.

"Then that's my Christmas, Clare. You, and the baby, and the taxes for another year—that's enough Christmas for anyone. More than enough for me."

Day 2: Lineage

"Clint Mathis, are you telling me you're not going to ask her?" Ellen fisted her hands on her hips and stared at her brother, who kept his gaze trained on the horses in the corral and didn't say a word. "I happen to know she's already turned down two fellas, and if a girl inviting you to come share lunch before you help her with the greenery isn't asking to be asked, I don't know what is!"

She deftly climbed the fence and perched on the top rail with her back to the horses, where she could see Clint's face. His attempted shrug didn't match the tight line of his lips or the pale cast to his cheeks that said he cared a lot more than he wanted to show. Slowly, her indignation drained away.

"Everybody's known you and Ruthie were a pair since your school days. What changed? And when? Just last week you were going to ask her."

"Never said that."

Ellen snorted.

"When a fella comes home after seeing a girl's blue dress and asks me to iron the blue shirt he hasn't worn in ages because the collar itches, you don't think I know what it means? What changed, Clint?"

"Nothing." The fact that he still wouldn't meet her eyes contradicted his words.

"Should I get Pa to come slap some sense into you?"

Glad Tidings

Though their father had never raised a hand to either of them in anger, Clint flinched a little, reflexively rubbing his jaw, and Ellen's heart sank.

"I didn't mean that. You know I didn't." She reached over and turned her brother's face a bit to examine the fading bruise, but something about the memory suddenly sat her up straight. "Clint, was it Les? Did he say something? Threaten something?"

"I can hold my own against Les, El." The quick way he turned his head so she couldn't see his eyes spoke volumes.

"I swear, two days on this ranch and that lowdown snake caused more trouble than—"

"Ellie…" His tone had switched back to the scolding big brother, and Ellen tried to douse the flame of anger in her chest.

"He did say something, didn't he?" The tension in Clint's shoulders tightened, proof she was on the right track, and her mind raced with possibilities. "Was that why you fought? Something about Ruthie?"

"Nope."

"Then what did he say to you?" The stubborn set of Clint's jaw said they could be at this all afternoon. Ellen slapped the rail next to her. "That's it. I'm going to town and ask Les."

Clint's lightning fast grip was around her wrist in an instant, and she caught one flash of the pain in his dark eyes before he looked away, dropping her hand as if it was a hot branding iron. The slump of his shoulders spelled defeat, and whatever the obstacle, she had never seen Clint Mathis give up.

"Clint, what did he say?" Ellen's voice was a whisper as she gently lifted her brother's chin.

"Just the truth." The words were almost too low to catch, but after a moment, he raised his eyes to hers again, and the raw pain cut into her soul. "Blood tells, Ellie."

Blood tells. She hadn't thought anyone in town still gave any thought to Clint's questionable parentage, at least since a stern lecture from the schoolteacher and a few pointed sermons from the minister. Most of the time even she forgot he hadn't been born her brother.

"Your pa might not have been one of the outlaws, Clint. More likely they picked you up in a raid somewhere. Maybe you've got rich relations out East, and they wanted you for ransom or something." She tried to speak lightly, but Clint gave a weary shake of his head, as though he'd been over every possible path a thousand times in his mind.

"Doesn't matter. I'll never know for sure, and how could I ask—a girl—to take that chance? Blood'll tell somewhere, and if it's bad…" He put his head down on top of his arms, and Ellen sat stunned for a moment with his words turning circles in her brain.

"Clint Mathis." Her voice was a little shaky, but it hardened into righteous determination as the answer finally came. "You're not what your pa was, whatever that might be. You've been adopted, you hear me? Twice. Maybe our family name isn't enough to wipe away your past, but you said it yourself. Blood tells. Are you going to stand here and tell me that Jesus' blood isn't strong enough to keep you from the wrong that might be in yours? That it's not strong enough for your kids and your grandkids and on down the line? There's only one bloodline that's not bent toward sin, and you got that the day you prayed. You think Reverend Dobbs and Ruthie can't see that? If they cared about any other kind of blood, they'd have told you long before this."

Slowly, Clint's head lifted, and wondering awe began to melt away the fearful questions in his eyes. Ellen gave his shoulder a playful push.

"Go wash your face and change into your blue shirt. There's a girl in town waiting to be asked to the Christmas social."

Day 3: Bethlehem

"Bethlehem, Katie. Beth-le-hem." I stressed every syllable, making a frantic dive for the pile of bathrobes lying on the armchair and trying not to lose my hold on the crumpled stack of papers clutched in my fist.

I mentally ran through the list of boys for the third time, confirming that Stanley Johnston was the only practical choice for a substitute head-shepherd, despite the eyeglasses that I had hoped to hide in the background, as Katie patiently began again, "Now when Jesus was born in Bethelham of Judaea…"

"Katie!" I would have clasped my hands to my head if either of them had been free. As if Orson Caldwell coming down with bronchitis and the Brewsters' dog ruining half the new set of angel wings wasn't enough, my sister's tongue had become inexplicably incapable of pronouncing the name of the city at the very heart of the pageant.

I threw a look at the clock, decided against buttoning my coat, and bundled myself and the pile of bathrobes into the car with Katie following close behind.

"Beth. Le. Hem. Hem, like the hem of a dress. Try again."

"Bethel—"

"Beth-le-hem."

"Beth-le-hem." Katie sounded it slowly and carefully, and I breathed a sigh of relief.

"Now say it in your piece."

Glad Tidings

"Now when Jesus was born in Bethelham of—"

"Oh, Katie!" I almost wailed. "Bethlehem. Hem! Keep practicing."

Katie dutifully started over, succeeding in one of every three attempts, and I tried desperately to remember how I had ended up in this mess. Of course no one expected Mrs. Stover to direct the Christmas pageant this year, barely a week after hearing of her youngest son's death in the Pacific, but how anyone had thought of giving me her place was a mystery too great to fathom. Teaching the nursery Sunday school was certainly no preparation for molding a crowd of fifty children—some only a few years younger than me—into something resembling a fitting memorial of the Lord's birth.

By the time we reached the church, Katie's accuracy had improved to two in three tries, and she had made it twice through her entire part with only a slightly halting rhythm to hint at her lingering uncertainty. I left her repeating, "Bethlehem. Bethelham. Bethle-hem," and plunged into a sea of children in every conceivable state of winter gear and biblical costume.

Before the choir began their first song, I had managed to piece out the new sets of angel wings with the least shabby of the old, use the extra robes from home to outfit two shepherds and an innkeeper who had forgotten their costumes, and make certain that no stray boots or mittens would mar the scene with an untimely appearance. I was beginning to feel rather proud of my success when a glance beyond the curtain revealed Mrs. Stover sitting on the very front pew, and the sight sent ice through my veins.

Not that I wasn't glad she'd come; if the Christmas pageant could bring her any comfort, I would be thankful, but the thought that she would be forced to watch my miserable attempt to follow in the steps she'd trod for over twenty years made my mind and body go numb in horror.

A touch on my arm alerted me that Sally Kobeck had not forgotten her cue if I had, and I stepped aside to let her pass, sweeping my eyes anxiously over Mary, Joseph, and the gray-flannel donkey that stood waiting nearby. With a deep breath and a firm resolve that I would not let anything mar this night for Mrs. Stover, I motioned them forward after Sally and ran to be sure that my wayward innkeeper had not forgotten his place as well as his costume.

I found myself holding my breath a number of times as the pageant progressed, but everything went off much more smoothly than I had expected. I managed to save Stanley's eyeglasses when they were knocked to the floor by some under-shepherd's wildly swinging crook; little Maisie Pettibone was only poked in the eye by another girl's wing after the angels had filed back behind the curtain; and when Dale Wallace was overcome with stage fright, his sister Dot stepped in to finish his part so naturally that no one could tell it hadn't been planned. I had just bent to fix the robe that was in danger of sending the third wise man toppling into the second and was congratulating myself that the last possible catastrophe had been averted when Katie stepped to the front of the stage and began to recite in a voice that carried clearly to every corner.

"Now when Jesus was born in Bethelham of Judaea…"

I froze in place, my eyes darting instinctively to Mrs. Stover. Her head went down on her hand, and she hid her eyes in her handkerchief. My heart dropped to my shoes, and I wanted nothing more than to slink away into the darkness, but like the dutiful captain of a sinking ship, I stayed at my post through the frantic rush to fling away costumes and claim the promised milk and cookies, the gratingly kind words from parents too wrapped up in their offspring's success to speak of my failure, the endless search for coats and boots and mittens.

As I tied the last hat on the last curly brown head, a hand touched my shoulder, and the soft but commanding voice I had hoped to escape spoke in my ear.

"A wonderful pageant, my dear."

"Oh, don't! It was horrid! You heard her. You must have. I tried so hard—" A choking lump rose in my throat, but when I raised my eyes to Mrs. Stover's, she was smiling through a film of tears.

"My Ben used to say it just that way. You brought him back to me tonight, if only for a moment." She bent to place a kiss on

Glad Tidings

Katie's cheek. "In all my years, I've never seen a more beautiful pageant."

Day 4: Inn

Kayla stepped back and surveyed the activity board with a critical frown. Did the flyer for the living nativity stand out well enough amid the clutter of less important holiday attractions? Perhaps if she moved the light parade to the bottom corner—but no, that would only draw people's eyes down to begin with, and they would never return for the rest. Best to leave it where it was.

She adjusted the tinsel that had drooped a bit over the mantel and returned to her desk, casting an eye around the lobby that Jen had somehow decorated to look just like a Hallmark movie set before sinking into her chair with a sigh.

The snug inn nestled in the quaint little town would have been perfect for a Hallmark movie. Only in a movie, it would have been complete with a bubbly, almost too friendly hostess, bearing trays of cookies and nuggets of grandmotherly wisdom, who would worm her way into the hearts of even the coldest guests and win them over to the true spirit of Christmas, or the charm of country life, or the blessing of family togetherness, or whatever the message of the week happened to be. Preferably while also opening their eyes to the love of their life, who just happened to run the bakery, or the Christmas tree stand, or the local sheriff's office.

Kayla couldn't help a little snort at the thought. While Chloe Magill at the bakery surely wouldn't mind a few more handsome men to flirt with, Ralph Nolton had sold the town's Christmas trees

Glad Tidings

for upwards of thirty years and couldn't be called ruggedly handsome by anyone's definition. And the local sheriff had inconsiderately chosen a local wife and three local children rather than waiting for the big city girl with a snobby attitude and a heart of gold who might one day have had her car break down while inexplicably taking a detour twenty miles from the interstate.

No, Kayla admitted to herself, it wasn't the lack of matchmaking material that made her lament her failure as a hostess. It was her own terrible shyness, the creeping certainty that any attempt to intrude herself into her guests' lives beyond answering questions and exchanging polite greetings would be seen as odd at best and insufferably rude at worst, the infuriating habit her brain had of only providing her the right thing to say at least five seconds after it would have made sense to say it.

Why had she thought any of that would change when she'd accepted Jen's offer to come and work at the inn? Maybe she was the one who needed some dashing guest or the local handyman to come sweep her off her feet and transform her from the creeping caterpillar into the graceful butterfly who brightened people's lives just by fluttering past.

But that was ridiculous. People in love didn't instantly transform into gushing founts of wisdom and helpfulness; if her experience was anything to go by, being in love would only make her more awkward and self-conscious than she already was. She braced her head in her hands and stared down at the old-fashioned ledger. Of course all the books were kept on the computer, but Jen had insisted that it added to the charm of the place, and the guests didn't seem to object. If only their hostess could be half so charming.

The desk phone beeped for an internal call, and her eyes scanned the guest book as she reached for the handset. Room 20, the Hudsons, a middle-aged couple with three adorable children. Should she greet them by name? Or was that too creepy?

"Desk speaking....No, ma'am, the drugstore closes at nine. Is there anything I can get you?...Yes, ma'am, I have some. I'll bring it right up....Of course, you're welcome."

Angie Thompson

Hurrying to a cupboard, Kayla rummaged for a bottle of cough syrup and quietly crept up the stairs to room 20, where a tired-looking Mrs. Hudson took the bottle with a quick word of thanks and closed the door. As Kayla made her way back down the greenery-lined stairs, her momentary glow of satisfaction faded into the old, nagging questions. Should she have done something more? Offered hot tea? Hard candies? Assured them that she would be manning the desk phone all night and they shouldn't hesitate to ring her up if they needed anything? She certainly couldn't call them back now.

Slumping into her chair, Kayla again scanned the list of names. The LaFontès, a beautiful young couple with an unstated tension simmering between them. Wasn't there some activity she could suggest that would begin to knit their hearts again? The Slighs and her mother, Mrs. Javitz, who always looked so tired when they came back from an all-day excursion. Would it be an unspeakable intrusion to propose that the older lady keep her company in the parlor some morning? Adrian Wilson, who was studying for the bar exam and scarcely poked his head out of his room long enough for the free breakfast. Would he take kindly to a cup of coffee brought to his door, or the suggestion of a walk in the fresh air to clear his head?

As yet another wave of frustration at her own uselessness swept over her, Kayla bent her head over the ledger and did the only and the best thing she could. She prayed.

Day 5: Stable

"Ain't exactly the way we planned on spendin' the night, is it, Tex?"

The horse thus addressed poked a soft black nose over the door of his stall and gently nipped at a battered hat that rested against a mound of hay. The hat fell back to reveal the face beneath it—a youthful face, but with an air that said its owner was no stranger to hard work and trouble.

"Oh, I know it ain't nothin' to you, boy." The young man smiled fondly as he reached up to stroke the silky muzzle. "You'd be in a barn as snug as this one in any case, though the little 'uns never did forget the animals Christmas mornin'. But it's a comedown from Christmas at home anyway, even if I oughta be thankful we found a roof of some kind."

The horse returned to his dinner, and his master shifted his position on the hay, wincing a bit as he did so.

"Ain't that I'm complainin' so much, Tex. Decent enough folks, seems like, and I sure wouldn't cotton to some no-account tramp sleepin' in the house with Ma and the girls around."

A little snort answered him, and the young man smiled.

"Well, no, I wouldn't call myself exactly that, though I'm no saint either, for a fact. But they got no way of knowin', nohow. Can't take chances with a stranger, that's all. It ain't the barn I'm objectin' to anyway. Not so much. But I did have such a hankerin' for Christmas at home."

Glad Tidings

Tex nickered softly in answer, and the young man folded his hands behind his head and lay back against the hay.

"You see, it's been more'n three years since I was back. Three Christmases at least, though no, I forgot—this one makes the fourth. And I don't know how it was—I just started feelin' that I'd like to be there again, for Christmas, and it kinda grew till I couldn't shake it. But I didn't reckon on my leg painin' me this bad, or I woulda started sooner."

The black neck arched out of the stall door again, and the young man waved his hand dismissively.

"It ain't that bad tonight. I gave it a good rub with some of that liniment, and it feels a sight better. Just can't ride as long or as hard as I used to, and that's what's done the mischief."

The horse's head disappeared once more, but after a moment, his master continued.

"Don't suppose you know what a Christmas is, Tex, horses never havin' such a thing. Though I seem to recollect that first Christmas happened in a stable of some kind. Never could figure why. I mean, sure, it makes sense to stick me in a barn, me bein' a man and a stranger and all. But what harm could a baby do?"

Tex seemed to have no reply to this, and the young man's tone grew thoughtful as he stared up at the rafters.

"My pa used to say somethin' about makin' Himself humble—the lowest of the low—so's we could know He felt all our pain, bein' as how he'd been there too. I never did quite understand it. Course, I never had to sleep in a barn either, before tonight."

An answering rumble brought a sheepish smile to the young man's face, and he gave a little sigh.

"Oh, I know it. I coulda slept in a bed and not kept you awake with my grousin' if I'd stopped in that little town a piece back like anyone with sense woulda done. I knew I didn't really have any chance of makin' it tonight. I just—" There was a moment of silence before his voice finally resumed. "Tell you what, Tex boy, I just had to try somehow. It ain't home, or anythin' close, but I got just as far as I could. I gave it my all tryin', see? Maybe those extra few miles don't mean nothin' to nobody else, but they're special to me. Givin' up before I give it everything I got—well, that ain't really tryin', Tex. Not to me."

Tex let out a soft breath, and his master closed his eyes, reaching for his hat as his voice gradually slowed.

"Wonder if that's what Pa meant by it. If maybe it was the same for Him…showin' us just how far He was willin' to come." The young man's hand reached up to tilt the hat brim over his eyes, and the motion held just the slightest tremor. The silence stretched long, but the horse remained still, his head cocked as if waiting, and his master's voice once more floated sleepily through the darkness.

"Wonder if Pa would read that old story again, Tex…for me…when we get home."

The horse stood for a minute longer until a soft snore proclaimed the young man asleep, then quietly returned to his hay.

Day 6: Child

"Mrs. Flannery?" Gwen's voice was five shades of apologetic, and I guessed what was coming before I even looked up from my desk. "Ross's sister seems to be running late, and I wouldn't mind, but I have an appointment…"

"You go ahead, Gwen." I raised my head in time to see the almond eyes peering worriedly from behind her and bit off a sharp comment that wasn't meant for his ears. "Ross can sit with me until she comes."

Gwen shot me a grateful look and hurried away, and I brushed my irritation into a corner where I could easily find it again and smiled up at the young man in the doorway.

"Why don't we wait outside, Ross? It's not too cold today."

"Yeah!" His face lit up like a string of leftover Christmas lights, and I quickly locked the office door and followed him to one of the chilly wrought-iron benches that sat on the porch. Gwen was too charitable by half, and I didn't intend to let Melissa Sanders waltz in as though she wasn't going on twenty minutes late without some indication that we weren't going to stand for it much longer.

"How was your Christmas, Ross?"

"Awesome!" He pulled his backpack into his lap and started tugging at the zipper. "Want to see?"

"Sure." I gave him an encouraging smile that he didn't notice, having his head buried in the backpack.

Glad Tidings

"I got one—two—three!" He pulled out a set of thin coloring books, the kind that came two to a pack at the dollar store, then began rummaging again. "And a whole big box this time!" He proudly displayed a standard 24-pack of crayons, then shoved it back into his backpack and bent to roll up his pant leg. "And new socks!" The plain white off-brand crew socks made the irritation in my chest flare hot again. The entire haul must have cost less than five dollars. Why couldn't some families see that just because their disabled relatives met small gifts with a child's eagerness didn't mean they didn't deserve anything better?

A beat-up sedan rounded the corner into the parking lot none too slowly, and a young woman with frizzy red hair and a rumpled server's uniform wrestled hurriedly with her seatbelt before finally releasing herself from the car.

"I'm sorry! I'm so sorry. Two of the kids came down with the stomach flu at the babysitter's, and I had to wait for my husband to get home, and they kept him ten minutes late, and then he got stuck in traffic…" Her excuses died off when they were met with silence, and she swallowed hard. "Anyway, I really am sorry."

"It's not fair to our staff to make them stay after hours, Mrs. Sanders. You need to pick Ross up on time or start making other arrangements."

"I know." The woman's voice was small. "I'm sorry." She raised her eyes to mine for just an instant, then dropped them again and turned to Ross. "We need to go, buddy. Did you have a good day?"

"Nope. A great day!" Ross straightened to his full five-foot height and wrapped his arms around his sister in a hug that must have taken her breath away. But even so, her stiff body lost some of its tension as she returned the embrace. "Oh, I made you something!" Ross let go with a jerk and dropped his backpack on the bench again, rummaging through it eagerly. "There!" He pulled out a page from one of the coloring books, neatly colored in three shades of blue.

"Aww, I love it, Ross. You want to put it up in your frame when we get home?"

"Yeah!" His face lit up again, and a little of its glow seemed reflected in hers for just an instant before her eyes caught me and immediately lost their sparkle.

"Come on, bud. We have to go. We can't keep people waiting, and I still have to make supper."

"Yeah! Spaghetti night!" Ross pumped his fist and knelt to zip up his backpack.

"Ahh, no, buddy. Not tonight." She grimaced, likely envisioning the combined effect of spaghetti and the stomach flu, and for once, I didn't blame her. "How about mac and cheese? You like that, right?"

"Love it!" Ross shot her an enthusiastic grin as he finally tugged the backpack closed, and his sister swallowed hard, pulling him into another hug.

"What would I do without you, big brother?" The words were spoken so low she couldn't have meant them for anyone else's ears, but my eyes jerked up to her face. It was softer than I had ever seen, and the flustered look she generally wore had melted into lines of weariness. In another instant, she straightened, motioning toward the car, and her face resumed its harried expression. "Come on, buddy. Mark can't take care of Gem and Trace and corral the rest of the kids for long."

"Can I help?" Ross asked eagerly, and his sister smiled again as they started down the stairs.

"Yep. You can help Lori and Ryder with their new coloring books and stop Max from eating the crayons while Mark and I make dinner and take care of the sick ones, okay?"

"Yes!" Ross pumped his fist, and I had to swallow a lump in my throat. How had I missed this? Why had I assumed neglect and indifference instead of grinding poverty and a caring if chaotic family struggling just to get by?

I watched until the car was out of sight, then returned to my desk, picking up the letter sitting in the printer on my way. Too many late pick-ups, too many late payments, failure to take part in extracurriculars, families on the waiting list who can make better

Glad Tidings

use of our services. The envelope sat stamped and waiting, addressed to Mrs. Melissa Sanders. I quietly signed the letter, folded it, ripped it in two, and filed it carefully away.

Day 7: Swaddling Clothes

"Mamá, what's wadding glows?"

I looked up from the pan I had just pulled from the oven to find Gina's frosting-covered fingers clutched around her picture Bible and shrugged my shoulders helplessly.

"Swaddling clothes, mija. It's how they used to dress little babies to keep them warm."

"Like footies?"

I laughed as I began scooping the cookies onto the cooling rack. "Not like footies. Like a big piece of cloth that you wrap all around the baby to hold them tight."

"Like a blankie?"

"Mmmm, better than a blankie." I slid the pan back onto the stove and knelt down next to her. "Blankies are nice, but when Mamá and Papá take their baby that they love sooo much"—I began acting out the words—"and they hold them in their arms, and they wrap them up so tight—oh, it makes the little babies feel so warm and safe!"

Gina giggled and struggled in my arms, and I let her go, brushing bits of frosting and dough from my apron as I stood and surveyed the job left to do.

"Okay, mija, we need to finish frosting these cookies if we want enough left to take to the station tomorrow after Papá eats them all."

Glad Tidings

Gina clambered back onto her sticky chair, but the ring of the doorbell sent her scrambling to the floor again with a cry of "Papá's home!"

I pulled off my apron and swiped at the flour on my face as I dashed after her, glancing at the clock without noticing the time in my rush. But when I opened the door, the bright red numbers and the sweat-soaked uniform and Gina's joyful call of "Uncle Chess!" hit me all at once, and my breath froze in my lungs.

* * *

It was hours later that my mamá's arm wrapped around my shoulders, careful not to disturb Gina, who was curled up in my lap, sucking her thumb like she hadn't for a year.

"How's Miguel?"

"I don't know. Well, I do, a little, but I only saw him for a minute. He broke some ribs and punctured a lung. There's some bruising on the inside. They want more x-rays of his leg. The guys have been taking turns with him, but Gina burst out crying when we walked in, and she won't go to Chester or anyone."

"Come, mija." Mamá knelt down in front of me and held her arms out to Gina with the tone in her voice that was both comforting and commanding. "Let Mamá go in and see Papá now."

Gina whimpered and burrowed deeper in my chest, but when Mamá gently lifted her into her own lap, she didn't break into screams, which was a major improvement over anyone else who had tried. She reached her arms out to me, and tears welled in her eyes, but Mamá only pulled her closer and continued speaking softly.

"Papá was hurt being a hero today, and it makes Mamá so sad not to see him. So Abuelita is going to sit with you, and Mamá is going to go in and see Papá, and she'll come back and tell us how Papá's doing before we go home." She gave me a firm nod to match her tone, and I obeyed, winding my way back through the halls to the room I'd had to leave so quickly a few hours ago. Two of the firefighters were standing outside the door, talking in low tones, but when I hesitated, they waved me ahead.

I crept in as silently as I could, trying to blink back tears at the sight of my strong Miguel lying on the bed, his tanned skin much too pale in the harsh light of the overhead bulbs, IVs and wires running from his arms and chest, an oxygen tube strapped to his face. I took a step closer, and he opened his eyes.

"How are you feeling, cariño?" I rubbed my thumb very gently over his cheek, and he gave me a smile that was too full of pain.

"I'm all right. You shouldn't worry." His voice was rough, and the words slurred together. "How's Gina?"

"Mamá has her. She's going to take her home as soon as I tell her how you are."

"You should go home and sleep. You look tired."

"Don't be silly, Miguel." I crossed my arms stubbornly, swallowing the lump in my throat. "You nearly got killed pulling a man from a burning building. Why should I go home and curl up in my bed?"

"You'll be cold. It's freezing here." He shivered, and I carefully rubbed his arm and pulled the thin hospital blankets a little closer. His eyes drifted shut, then suddenly opened again. "Oh. The present. From my car. I asked Chester—to bring it in."

"Shhh." I put a finger softly to his lips. "Presents can wait till you're feeling better."

"Not this one. I want you—to have it tonight."

"Miguel—"

"Please."

I never could resist his eyes when they begged that way, and especially not tonight. I found the box sitting under a chair and brought it to Miguel's bedside, carefully pulling off the paper and wishing my baby wasn't so scared when I saw the label, "To Papá, Mamá, and Gina." I lifted the lid, and the tears spilled over.

"Oh, Miguel!"

Inside were three matching bathrobes covered with hearts and snowflakes, the ones Miguel had laughed at when I saw them in the store.

Glad Tidings

"For Christmas Eve. To keep us all warm."

I leaned over and kissed his cheek under the tubing, then I took the largest robe from the box and tucked it gently around him before slipping my own over my clothes and letting the softness wrap me like a hug. Then I gathered the little one close to my chest and looked down at Miguel again.

"I'll be back, cariño. There's a little girl who needs her papá to wrap her up *so* warm and safe."

Day 8: Manger

"Very, very quiet, Nora."

"Krissie's sleeping?" Her little sister's whisper was still too loud, but at least she was trying.

"No, she's not sleeping, but she's very, very sick today."

"Why come the medicine makes her sick?"

"Because…" Their mother's voice trailed off as she reached for an explanation that would satisfy the inquisitive four-year-old. "Because the medicine has to make the bad stuff really sick so it'll go away and leave Krissie alone. But when it makes the bad stuff sick, it makes Krissie sick too."

"But Krissie will get better and the bad stuff won't?"

"That's what we're hoping, Norie." Even for Nora's sake, her mom couldn't lie.

"I want her to get better, Mommy."

"I know it, sweetie. We all do."

"I can lay with her?"

"Probably not today, sweetheart."

Kris finally managed to pry her eyes open a crack and meet the little worried ones peering up at her. With what felt like superhuman effort, she moved her hand enough to feebly pat the bed twice before closing her eyes again.

"Are you sure, sweetie?" Her mom bent over her, carefully stroking her head, and Kris wanted to cry. Her mom was only trying to help, but it made things so much harder when she had to insist

Glad Tidings

rather than being believed the first time. But sick or not, she and her sister needed each other. She licked her lips, swallowed down the queasy feeling in her throat, and finally managed to force the word out.

"Yeah."

Her mom sighed.

"Very, very still, Norie. If Krissie starts feeling worse with you up here, I'll have to take you down, understand?"

Nora must have nodded because her mom lifted her to the bed and settled her carefully under Kris's arm. Her little sister's body was uncomfortably warm against her, but the feel of the chubby little arm tucked snugly beneath hers was comforting enough to help her fight the wave of nausea that threatened to rise again. Nora lay entirely still, and after a few minutes, the soft rise and fall of her chest and the quiet rhythm of her heartbeat finally lulled her sister to sleep.

* * *

When Kris woke again, the light had shifted a little, but Nora still lay curled up beside her in the hospital bed. Kris let her eyes roam the room, thankful that the awful sick feeling wasn't quite as bad as earlier, until she found her mother sitting in the corner. The minute she saw Kris was awake, she stood up and came closer, still speaking in a hushed voice.

"How are you feeling, sweetie?"

"Better." Her voice sounded weak even in her own ears.

Her mom reached for the glass on the table and held the straw to her lips.

"Try just a sip, sweetheart."

Kris obeyed, and although the tiny bit of water sloshed uncomfortably in her stomach, it cleared her head a little.

"Norie's still here?"

"She made something she wanted to show you, so she didn't want to leave until you woke up, and then she fell asleep. I think all the cousins at Grammy's wore her out."

The lump that rose in Kris's throat this time had nothing to do with her stomach.

"I'm missing all the best parts of Christmas."

"I know, sweetheart." Her mom's voice sounded almost as choked as her own. "Next year. Next year it'll be better than ever."

If she had a next year. Kris drew a shuddering breath, and Nora suddenly shifted beside her. Her round, blue eyes blinked for a second, and she almost sat up but seemed to remember in time.

"You feel better, Krissie?"

"A little bit. Thanks for helping, Norie."

Nora wiggled around to face her and planted a little wet kiss on her sister's cheek.

"I can show you what I drawed now?"

"Sure."

Nora reached into the pocket of her red and green plaid jumper and pulled out a sheet of red construction paper that had been folded into a wad to fit the tiny space. She sat up and unfolded it on the pillow, smoothing it carefully with her chubby hands.

"See?"

Their mom reached over and held up the picture at an angle where Kris wouldn't have to crane her neck, and she studied it carefully. A little white blob with a face and one of Nora's signature girl stick figures sat inside a roughly rectangular brown outline with yellow scribbled all around them. The puzzle was too much for her tired brain, and she shook her head.

"What is it, Norie?"

"It's baby Jesus in a manger!"

"Oh." If the little white blob had been alone, maybe she could have guessed. "Is that Mary in the manger with Him?"

Nora shook her head.

"Prentiss said a manger was a dirty food box for horsies, and I asked Grammy why they put baby Jesus in a dirty food box and not in a nice bed. And Grammy said 'cause they couldn't be at home where the nice bed was, and the manger was a little nasty, but people and horsies couldn't step on Him there, so they could keep Him

Glad Tidings

safe till He could go back home again. And I said kind of like Krissie can't come home now, but the doctors are keeping her safe till she's better again? And Grammy started crying and hugged me and didn't say yes, but I thinked it was kind of the same, so I drawed you in the manger too."

Silent tears were streaming down Kris's face by the time Nora finished, and she reached shaking arms out and hugged her sister hard.

"And Krissie?" Nora's voice whispered close in her ear. "I know you're gonna get better. That's why I drawed your hair."

Day 9: Shepherds

"Blamed ol'—"

"Stuff it, Rand. It won't help. Just keep watch." Kane Daniels stepped back from the rocky shelf overlooking the road and dropped to where his youngest brother lay gasping for breath with their cousin bending over him. "How's it look, Micah?"

"Ain't good. I can keep him from bleedin' to death for a while, but that's about it. He needs a doctor bad."

"And just how do you figure on gettin' one if the whole town's after us?" Rand's words hissed from above them.

"You keep your eyes on that road and leave this to me." Kane shot him a stern look, and Rand swallowed a retort and turned back to his post. This was as hard on Rand as anyone, but Kane couldn't let his hot-headed brother go off half-cocked or he'd end up as bad as Luke, or worse.

"Tell me again what they said, little brother." He wiped the sweaty hair from Luke's forehead and held the canteen to his lips. Luke gulped the water gratefully, coughing and moaning as his battered ribs protested.

"Somethin' about—old Tom Donahue. How we—burned his house and—come nigh to killin' him. And the usual about—gettin' our filthy sheep off—Carson County land."

"It don't make no sense. We ain't been near the Donahue place in weeks."

Glad Tidings

"Makes sense if it ain't really about old Tom." Micah's voice was low as he glanced toward the shelf.

"Meanin' they're tryin' to run us out, and this is a good excuse." Micah nodded, and Kane ran a hand over his face.

"Well, they mighta got what they're aimin' for."

"Kane, no." Luke's words were a moan, and Kane gripped his shoulder. "You can't just—let 'em win."

"I'm as stubborn as the next man and a sight more'n most, but seein' my kin beat and shot up for a few head of sheep is a bit farther'n I'm willin' to go."

"You know that 'few head of sheep' is all we got in the world." Micah looked up from the bandage he'd just tied off and met Kane's eyes steadily.

"Don't think I don't. But it ain't worth none of your lives. We can't go much farther out than Carson if we plan to keep an eye on Meredith, but I'd rather sweep floors in the mercantile than hold those sheep over one of your graves."

"Kane, we got trouble."

Kane was at Rand's side in an instant, instinctively drawing his gun, and his brother pointed.

"Sheriff and one other."

Even from a distance, there was no mistaking the large man and his big bay. Kane gritted his teeth. In his concern over Luke's attackers, he had barely registered the severity of the charge. How many would testify against them out of spite? Or would they even make it to trial? He'd known more than one posse to appoint itself judge, jury, and executioner on the spot.

Kane held the grip of his revolver tight for a few seconds, then slid it along the rock toward Rand, and his brother looked up with startled eyes.

"What are you doin'?"

"What I have to." He quickly unbuckled his gun belt and turned to look his brother in the eye. "Let the sheriff in, but don't let anyone else get close. I'm gonna bargain for a doctor for Luke, but you make sure they don't sneak a posse in, hear?"

"Bargain what?" The edge of fear in Rand's voice said he already knew. Kane grasped his shoulder.

"Luke's life's in our hands, little brother. You do your job, and I'll do mine. I'm countin' on you."

Rand dropped his head onto the rock, and Kane could see his gun hand trembling, but after a few seconds, he looked up again with a determination all the more fierce for the pain in his eyes.

"You do what you have to, Kane, but I ain't lettin' it end like this."

"Stay inside the law, hear? If you get yourself arrested or shot and leave Luke and Micah defenseless, I ain't never forgivin' you."

"I hear you." The words were forced through his teeth, sign enough that he recognized the truth of what Kane was saying. With one last cuff to Rand's arm, Kane dropped to the ground again and motioned to Micah.

"I'm gettin' Luke a doctor. Stay holed up somewhere till he can ride, and then either sell the sheep or get out of the county."

"Let me." As usual, Micah didn't have to be told what he was planning. Kane gripped his cousin's arm hard.

"Not happenin'. I'm still boss of this outfit. Rand'll take care of Luke if it comes to that. You're the only brother Merry's got."

"This ain't right, Kane."

"Best I can do. Hold Luke down, will you?"

Micah squeezed his eyes shut and gave a sharp nod.

"Daniels!" The sheriff's voice boomed through the canyon. "You boys in there?"

Kane waited until Micah reached Luke's side, then stepped out from behind the bluff with his hands raised.

"I'm comin' quiet, sheriff! The other boys had no hand in it. I'll give myself up if you'll send in a doctor for Luke."

Luke's cry of protest sounded faintly above the pounding in his ears. The sheriff rounded the bend and drew to a stop, surveying him with a curious smile.

"You gonna set your word up against old Tom's, son?"

"What's that?"

Glad Tidings

"Donahue came to, and he swears to hearin' the Holt boys set the fire and brag how they'd pin it on you. Doc rode along with me. Give me your word nobody'll start shootin', and I'll send him in."

Kane's knees suddenly went weak, and he leaned hard against the bluff.

"Sheriff—" A sudden memory of Luke's reason for riding into town washed over him, and he offered a shaky grin. "You don't look like no angel I ever heard tell of, but I reckon that's the second-best news anybody's ever brought a passel of sheepherders Christmas day."

Day 10: Night

Worst. Christmas. Ever.

It wasn't just the midnight asthma attack, or Dametrie sneaking out the window again after he thought I was asleep. Those were bad enough, but the look on Dad's face when he heard me coughing and came in to find Dametrie gone told me that things could only get worse from here.

Dad didn't ask me anything, whether because he wanted me to rest or just thought I didn't know, I couldn't tell. I knew a lot more than either of them probably thought, but I wasn't sure if I wanted to tell it. In a way, I was glad that somebody besides me knew about Dametrie, but I could see from the look on Dad's face as he sat by the wall that he was working up to the grandmother of all the fights they'd had since Dametrie started high school.

I closed my eyes, but there was no way I was going back to sleep. My own heavy breathing was the only sound for a long time, but finally there was a little scraping noise on the fire escape, and the window creaked open, not quite as carefully as usual.

Dametrie crawled back into the room and dropped down on the edge of his bed, coughing a little and breathing heavier than I was. I opened my eyes a tiny crack to see him wrestling with a wet pair of gloves and fumbling with the buttons of his snow-covered coat.

"Where you been?" Dad's voice was deadly calm, but Dametrie jumped and spun around, starting to shake like I'd never seen. Dad stood up where he still towered over him, but his next words

Glad Tidings

weren't the ones I expected. "Boy, you're soaked to the skin! Get out of those clothes before you catch your death."

Dad left the room, slamming the door behind him, and Dametrie obeyed as well as he could, shivering harder every minute. He'd managed to pull on a pair of sweats and a hoodie when Dad came back in with a mug that smelled like apple cider. He handed it to Dametrie, then pulled his legs up onto the bed and slipped dry socks on his feet without waiting for his help. Dametrie's teeth chattered against the mug, and Dad piled his own blankets and the couch blanket on top of him, pulling them up to his chin when Dametrie put down the mug and laid back.

For a long minute, there was no sound except Dametrie's coughing and shivering, but when it slowed a little, Dad's voice spoke again.

"How long you been sneaking out?"

Dametrie murmured something I couldn't catch. If he was honest, the answer was a week.

"And whatever you got going on is worth scaring Jayson and me to death and giving yourself pneumonia?"

This time there was no answer.

"Who you been going with, Dametrie?"

"Nobody."

"Why don't I believe that?"

"You don't believe nothing I say anymore."

I pressed my eyes shut. For just a minute, when Dametrie seemed so weak and Dad seemed so worried, I had hoped that maybe things would be better.

"If I can't even trust you to stay in the house when you're supposed to be asleep, how am I supposed to take your word?"

"You stopped trusting me a long time ago." Dametrie coughed again, and his bed creaked as he probably rolled on his side so he couldn't see Dad. I squinted my eyes open and caught a little glimpse of Dad's face, for once looking more sad than angry.

"You know I did a lot to mess up my life as a kid. I don't want to see you boys go down that path."

"I'm not!" Dametrie snapped, but there was hurt in his voice, and his next words were so low I almost didn't hear them. "I wish you'd listen."

"Tell me where you were tonight, Dametrie."

Dametrie drew a deep breath that still sounded shivery.

"I was at Mr. Howard's."

"You have something to do with that vandalism?" Dad's voice went stern again, and Dametrie groaned.

"No! Why would you think that? I was—" He broke off, coughing harder, and Dad helped him sit up and handed him the mug again. Dametrie took a drink and put his head down on his knees. "He was going to take that old nativity down, Dad. After whoever it was smashed up the sheep and camel. I told him if he left it up—I'd make sure nothing happened to it."

"You telling me the truth, son?"

"That old display means a lot to the kids around here. You ever seen how much Jay loves it? You really think I'd smash it up like that?" If I didn't know better, I'd have almost thought Dametrie was going to cry.

"So you been doing what?"

"Sitting out there with a flashlight to scare off anybody who might come back."

"You have any idea how dangerous that could have been, Dametrie?" I'd never heard Dad sound so scared. "What would you do if a gang showed up? Take them on yourself?" There was silence for a minute before he spoke again. "Why didn't you tell me?"

"Didn't think you'd care."

"Why?" Now it was Dad's voice that sounded like crying.

"When I told you about the vandals, all you did was lecture me about hanging out with the wrong crowd. I don't know who did it, Dad! And I sure wouldn't stick with them if I did."

"Son." Dad stopped and swallowed something in his throat. "I'm sorry. I guess—I guess I got to seeing you—well, seeing you as me at your age. I'll—I'll try to listen better. Try to see you for you. I won't be perfect. Can you work with me?"

Glad Tidings

Dametrie didn't answer, but after a minute, he put his arms around Dad, and Dad hugged him hard. I closed my eyes and drew a deep breath.

Best. Christmas. Ever.

Day 11: Flock

David Fowler reached hesitantly for the knob on his parents' door, feeling a faint jolt of surprise when it gave under his hand. He cautiously poked his head in to be met with soft exclamations from his family, who still sat around the flickering gas log in the living room.

"Thought you'd all be in bed by now." He accepted his mother's hug as he sank into a corner of the couch.

"We thought we'd stay up for a while." His dad didn't say it, but it was obvious they'd held out some faint hope for him. "Didn't figure you'd be driving this time of night."

"Hoped maybe I could sneak a piece of pie while no one was looking." David managed a grin as he stretched his legs in front of him.

"Sorry you missed the kids." His sister gave him a rueful look. "Want to go up and see them?"

"No way am I taking the blame for child crankiness on a six-hour drive. I'll give them a whirlwind hello-goodbye in the morning. Oh, almost forgot. Presents are in the car." He moved to stand, but his brother-in-law held out a hand.

"You look about dead on your feet, Dave. Give me your keys."

David handed them over thankfully, and Adam disappeared through the door as Mom hurried in from the kitchen with a cup of re-warmed chocolate. David saluted her with the mug and took a sip, letting his eyes slide closed as the warm drink relaxed his tight

39

Glad Tidings

muscles. Adam came back with the stack of gifts and set them in the nearly bare space under the tree, but no one made a move to open them.

"Rough day?" Dad asked, and David gave a combination sigh and chuckle.

"I knew I was signing up for it. Just didn't know it would all break loose on Christmas. I don't regret it; just sorry I missed you all."

"We missed you too." Mom dropped a kiss on his hair and began gently rubbing his shoulders. "Anything you can talk about? You said a car accident?"

"Oh, the car accident was just the end of it." David sighed and ran his fingers through his hair. "I told you I offered Riley a lift to the airport. Well, I had just dropped him off and was headed for the highway when I got a call from Phil Rodenham. They'd been up visiting Mel's dad and were supposed to fly back today, but he had emergency surgery last night—heart—and Mel didn't feel right leaving her sister alone. Which left Phil's mom alone in the nursing home over Christmas, and he wondered if I'd have any time to go see her."

"Of course you couldn't say no to that." Mom squeezed his shoulders, and he patted her hand as she returned to her chair.

"It wasn't a big thing, but I did—kind of underestimate how long Mrs. Rodenham can talk. Every time I started to excuse myself, she'd have something else to tell me about when Phil was a boy or her Christmases growing up in Georgia. Maybe I should've cut her off at some point, but—she was just so lonely. Anyway, the staff finally came to take her to lunch, and I started over here again, but Heather Lucas called, just about frantic. Cole lost his job a couple months back and—hasn't been doing well. He was—well, he wasn't in a good place."

"Did you go over there?" Dad's tone was soft with understanding, and David nodded.

"After I'd talked to him on the phone for close to an hour. But I think—I hope it helped. He gave me the pills, and he's going to come in for counseling starting Monday."

"Praise the Lord," Amber breathed, and David nodded.

"Just pray God'll give me the words to say."

"You know I will."

"So." David sighed. "That put me well past lunch. But I was actually almost halfway here when I got the call from Jim Mulligan."

"That was the car accident?"

"Yeah. Sherry was driving, but Trish was hurt pretty bad. Drunk driver ran through a stop sign." David swallowed hard. "It was touch and go for a while, but they have her stable now. Keep their family in prayer. And—" He bit his lip and shook his head. "Well, it'll be all over the news tomorrow, and I know you won't broadcast it. Pray for the Winters." He drew a deep breath. "It was Elliot in the other car."

"Oh, poor Beth!" His mother's hand flew to her mouth, and David clasped his hands tightly.

"Yeah. She took it hard. He was banged up pretty bad. Sobered up too. Someone told him he'd killed the little girl. I've never seen anyone so broken."

"You talked to him?" Adam's voice was hushed.

"Lionel and Beth saw me praying with the Mulligans. They weren't even going to ask until we heard that Trish was stable."

"I can imagine," Mom breathed, and Amber wiped away tears.

"He knows he's messed up his life good and proper this time. But I got the feeling he was listening—really listening—for the first time in a long time. They kicked me out to take him down to surgery, but he asked me to come again."

"You think God'll get hold of his heart?" Amber's voice held a thread of hope, and David closed his eyes and rested his head back.

"I pray He will."

Silence fell over the group, and David thanked God that he knew his family was praying.

"Well, Dave." Dad stood and crossed to his side, resting a strong hand on his shoulder. "Not the day any of us planned, but just keep in mind who it was the angels gave the first Christmas message."

Glad Tidings

"The lowest and poorest." David's mouth curved up in a tired half-smile. "I've remembered that all day."

"True, but not what I was thinking, son. That first good news was trusted to the men who kept the flock."

Day 12: Glory

Greg turned the corner by the high school, whistling a Christmas tune, and grinned when he saw Cathy Shaunessy's red hat bobbing up ahead. Lengthening his strides, he fell into step beside her, motioning nonchalantly to the bag she carried.

"Getting some last-minute practice?"

"I'll have you know I'm coming from the library, Greg Brooks! I have the music down pat, thank you very much. Unlike some people who still go flat on the second line of—"

"Say, won't the kids' faces be great tonight?" Greg quickly cut her off, firm in the belief that aspersions only half-cast didn't have to be answered to. The mischievous spark in Cathy's eye didn't fade, but she let him take her bag, and they were soon engaged in a friendly debate over which songs the children would appreciate most.

When they reached Maple, Debbie Robbins hailed them from the fence, and they were just saying their see-you-tonights when a whoop turned all eyes toward the corner as Tim Finley ran up at a breakneck pace, then bent over with his hands on his knees.

"Watch yourself, Timmy; I can't carry your part and mine if you lose your voice sucking cold air." Greg eyed his friend curiously, taking in the rumpled appearance that said he'd been running long before he caught sight of them.

"You should be—so lucky!" Tim gasped out, and Debbie tossed her head saucily.

Glad Tidings

"Why, Cath, I thought Greg could carry the whole quartet if he had to, and we were just up there to make the thing look good!"

Cathy laughed, and Tim finally straightened, sending the rest of the group a beaming smile.

"Did you hear? Mason Phelps has tonsillitis!"

"Oh, Tim, that's awful!" Cathy gasped, but Tim shook his head.

"Well, awful for him maybe. And for Southmore. But it's our big break!"

"How?" Debbie leaned in eagerly.

"No way they can sing at St. Matthew's tonight. So they called us! Well, they called Professor Hammond. And he called us—or at least, called me, and I said I'd round you up faster than he could get you on the phone."

"Awfully humble of you," Greg muttered, but Cathy clasped her hands.

"St. Matthew's wants us? Truly?"

"Why not? We came in second, didn't we? Ought to have won if—"

"Oh, skip all that, Tim!" Debbie cut him off before he could start on the second-cousin's-half-brother's-uncle connection he'd dredged up between one of the judges and the soprano in the Southmore quartet. "The candlelight service at St. Matthew's! That's the absolute top! What time should we be there? Do we have time to practice? You know you came in sharp on that last chorus…"

Greg let the talk continue without hearing it as his brain seemed to spin in circles. St. Matthew's drew crowds from around the state and beyond, and for a few local singers, it had been a stepping stone to unimaginable opportunities. He'd dreamed of a day like this, and yet…

"Greg?"

He snapped back to reality and realized that the others were watching him oddly.

"What did you say?"

"Why don't we meet for practice at the school at six and walk over from there?" Tim eyed him expectantly, and Greg swallowed hard.

"I—I can't."

"Well, say six thirty, then."

Greg slowly shook his head, and Cathy touched his arm.

"Greg, what's wrong?"

"I—" He instinctively moved a step back. "Have you forgotten? We're supposed to sing at the children's ward tonight."

Cathy's eyes went wide, but Debbie's face remained blank.

"Well, sure, but that was before." Tim looked bewildered.

"Didn't we give our word we'd be there? Haven't they told the kids we're coming?"

"Things happen. They'll understand that." Debbie's voice was coaxing, and Greg looked away.

"If one of *us* had come down with tonsillitis, sure. But we didn't. We're still perfectly fit and able. It's just that we've been asked to sing someplace else. They don't need us at St. Matthew's. They can get anyone they want. Don't you see? We'd be doing it for us, not for them."

"What's so wrong with wanting to sing at St. Matthew's?" Tim crossed his arms defiantly.

"Nothing. If we'd won it in the first place—or never promised anywhere else—then I'd be over the moon. But this—letting down those little kids to get our shot at glory— I'm sorry. I can't."

"But Greg, you wanted this so bad." Debbie reached out a hand as though to draw him back. "Remember the tenor who did the candlelight service three years ago?"

The fire of a dream ignited with her words, and he took a deep breath as he watched it crumble to ashes.

"Yes, and I remember the year I broke my leg and had to stay in the hospital over Christmas. If we hadn't promised, it would be different. But we did. And I'm going, even if I go alone. You'll have to find another tenor."

Greg turned and walked resolutely down the street, blinking back the mist that blurred his vision, steeling himself against the sound of running footsteps. An arm was thrust through his, but

Glad Tidings

Cathy didn't try to stop him, just kept pace with him until he realized his long strides were winding her. He stopped and turned to face her.

"I'm sorry, Cathy. I just can't."

"I never asked you to. I just want to know what time you're picking me up. Besides, you have my books."

He opened his mouth to answer, but a shout turned them around to see Tim running up.

"It's no good, Tim."

"Forget that! Think we've got time to train a new tenor? Deb's calling Professor Hammond, and we'll meet up at your place. If we're singing for a bunch of little kids tonight, at least I'm not letting them laugh at us when you go flat."

Tim turned to rush back toward Debbie's, and Greg swallowed the lump in his throat and pulled Cathy's arm tighter as they continued down the street.

Day 13: Angels

"Come on, Meggie; please come with me." Tasha knew she was begging, but that was the entire point. "You don't have to do anything but help me carry boxes. And you'll have fun. I know you will." *I've got to get you out of this house, girl.*

Megan stared dully past her through a pair of red-rimmed eyes that proclaimed clearly that she'd spent the whole day curled up on the sofa, crying over Kevin again.

Such a jerk. He doesn't even deserve her.

"Come on, Meg. You helped me shop for these. I don't want you to miss out on the fun."

"I don't feel like going out tonight." Megan shuddered, and her voice was flat, but talking was a huge improvement over not talking. Tasha gently pressed her advantage.

"What else are you gonna do, sweetie? You've seen all the Christmas reruns at least three times by now. And there's not a scoop of ice cream left in the house."

"Probably just go to bed. I've got a headache."

I'll bet you do. And crying yourself to sleep at seven at night is just going to mean you wake up at three in the morning with a worse one.

"Meggie, please. I know it's hard." Tasha sat down at the kitchen table and took her friend's hand, wincing inwardly as her conscience gave a little twinge. *Okay, so I've never had a boyfriend, let alone a bad breakup, but I moped around the house for a week*

Glad Tidings

when I was cut from swim team. That counts, right? "You have to start trying. You can't let—" Kevin's name was on her lips, but she caught herself in time. "—everything that's happened take away the wonderful, joyful, helpful girl I know is still in there."

Megan sighed.

"Can you do it another night? I'm *really* tired, Tasha."

Did she actually just agree to come? Tasha tried hard to keep too much hope from bleeding into her voice.

"There is no other night. They have to be delivered by Wednesday, and I'm working nursery that night. And Bible study's tomorrow."

"And why do you need me again?"

Yes, girl, come on, please!

"It's a lot of packages and probably a lot of stairs. And I really want you to see the kids' faces. Hour and a half max. Then I'll bring you straight home. I promise."

Megan bit her lip and closed her eyes, and Tasha tried one last offer.

"I'll let you stop for ice cream on the way home."

Megan threw a wistful glance at the empty freezer, and her shoulders slumped.

"Then you'll let me go to bed?"

"On my honor."

"Fine."

Oh, God, please! Tasha breathed the prayer as Megan stumbled toward her bedroom. *Please let tonight be what she needs.*

* * *

"Why are they called angel gifts again?" Megan's voice was still listless as she stared out the car window, poking her spoon in her sundae, but even the tiny spark of interest in her question was more than she'd shown in days.

"I don't know. Maybe we're supposed to be the angels—messengers of God's love, you know. Or maybe it's that verse about showing love to strangers and 'angels unaware,' right? Like you never know for sure if the person you stop to help is really an angel in disguise."

Megan snorted a little.

"Really loud angels, then." She rubbed her temples, and Tasha felt a little pang of remorse.

"Wasn't it awesome seeing the looks on their faces, though? And wasn't the baby the cutest?"

She had her eyes on the road, but Megan's sniff alerted her, and she glanced over to see a tear sliding down her friend's cheek.

"Kevin had a dimple like that." She buried her face in her hands, and Tasha's hope crumpled.

Really, Lord? The dimple? That's what she had to notice?

Swallowing back her sigh, she turned the car onto their street, and the flashing lights in front of them made her stomach go cold.

"Meg!" She hissed the word, and Megan looked up, her tears retreating in her shock.

"What's going on? Tasha, that's our house!"

"I don't know." Tasha parked in front of the neighbor's and peered out at the three squad cars blocking their driveway. Megan moaned and covered her eyes, and Tasha didn't blame her. The flashing lights were enough to give anyone a headache, let alone intensify an existing one.

Lord, why tonight? Why one more thing?

An officer approached their car, and Tasha rolled down the window.

"Is there a problem, officer? That's our house!"

"Can I get your name, please?"

Groaning inwardly, Tasha provided her own and Megan's information as the officer took notes.

"Looks like you had a burglary tonight, ma'am. One of your neighbors saw a suspicious van in the driveway and called 911. We picked up one suspect at the end of the street, but no sign of the van yet. As soon as the evidence team is through, we'll need you to take a look and tell us if anything's missing."

"Of—course." Tasha forced the words through dry lips.

Glad Tidings

"You have anywhere else you can stay for the night? Looks like they broke a window in the back bedroom getting in, so you'll want to get that fixed."

Back bedroom. Tasha's heart froze.

"We'll—yes. We'll find somewhere. Thank you."

"Wait here a minute. I'll go see if they're ready for a walkthrough."

She watched as the officer strode away, then turned to Megan, whose eyes were wide and staring.

"My bedroom?" Her voice was a whisper, but she didn't burst into tears again.

Her bedroom. If she hadn't gone with me—if she'd been home in bed with the lights out—

"Meggie." The word quivered on Tasha's lips. "I don't think *we* were the angels tonight."

Day 14: Fear Not

"Evan..." The word wavered beneath the ominous hissing of the car. "You said I shouldn't be afraid. You said it would be okay. You promised!"

Tess's brother didn't answer—understandable when he was thirty miles away and laid up with a broken ankle. He'd assured her she could do this. She knew the way to the lodge; the roads were well sanded; there was nothing to be afraid of. So easy for him to say! But her usual nagging worries were nothing compared to the terror that now engulfed her, watching steam pour from under the hood on a dark, desolate mountain road with no sign of help for miles, even if she could have forced herself out of the car to get to it.

She tapped her phone with shaking fingers. No bars, just like the last three times. She dialed anyway, hoping against all sense that it would somehow go through. Nothing.

"Evan!" Tears welled in her eyes, and she pulled her knees up and clutched them to her chest. "What am I supposed to do?"

Hot tears spilled over and ran down her cheeks, accentuating the chill of her skin. The heat hadn't worked all afternoon. How long did it take someone to freeze to death? How long before Evan realized she was in trouble?

Snowflakes drifted between the branches, beautiful and deadly. What if it got too deep for a search party? What if it buried her car? What if they never found her at all?

Glad Tidings

"Evan, I can't do this!" Choking sobs engulfed her, and her thoughts finally found their way beyond her brother to One who could truly help. "God, please! Please get me out of this! Please do—something!"

Fear not.

The words of the speaker's message floated softly through her mind, and she shook her head desperately.

"God, I know I'm—too fearful in the best of times. But even You have to admit that I have a right to be scared here. This is bad. Really bad. I need—some way to call Evan. Or the car to start working. Or something. Please!"

Fear not.

"God, this isn't helping! I can't *not* fear right now, and even if I could, what good would it do? You're not telling me the car senses fear or something?" Tess choked somewhere between a sob and a hysterical laugh. "Please, God, get me out of this! I'll—I'll try. I promise."

A faint buzzing noise pierced her senses, and Tess jerked her legs back to the floor, scanning the darkened dashboard for any sign that something was about to explode. But then a light appeared on the switchback above her, and she sucked in a breath of hope so deep it was almost painful.

"Is that a car? Please let it be a car!" Should she get out and wave her arms? Or would that just get her run over? "Please, please let them stop!"

The buzzing grew into roaring, and light swept the road before coming to a stop behind her. Tess stared into her mirror, and her heart froze in horror. A burly man with a bald head, long beard, and dark leather jacket dismounted his motorcycle and walked around to her door. Tess scrambled to double-press the locks before the biker knocked on her window.

"You wanna pop your hood?" The man yelled the words through the closed door, and Tess trembled. Should she? But he couldn't leave her any more stranded than she was. She found the release, and he disappeared behind the hood.

After a minute, he returned and motioned for her to roll the window down. It was all Tess could do not to shriek. What would he do to her if she gave him an opening? Why had God let this happen? The thought of being left alone again was only slightly more terrifying than the man who now stood in front of her, but on the trembling strength of that *slightly*, she opened her window the barest crack.

"You got a coolant leak. Could be a hose or your radiator. I can get you into town, but you should have someone take a look when you get back." He gave her a nod and walked to his bike, opening something and taking out a large jug. Returning to the front of her car, he fiddled for another minute before slamming the hood. Tess's hands were shaking so badly that she could barely turn the key, but somehow she managed it, and the car sprang to life again. Slowly, she inched back onto the road and continued down the mountain.

The motorcycle followed her—disconcerting but not surprising since it was a narrow road and the main route to anywhere, but when she reached the highway, the biker didn't move to pass her. Tess's fingers clutched the wheel tighter, her anxiety rising as the miles crawled by. What did he want from her? Would he follow her all the way home? Of course Evan would try to protect her, but what could he do with a broken ankle? And how long could she trust the fix for the engine to last?

Swallowing hard, she pulled onto the exit that would take her home, and the motorcycle revved its engine and sped past her into the night.

As she drove the few remaining blocks in silence, Tess's worry melted to shame. Apparently all the man had wanted was to see her make it to safety. And that after she had cowered in her car without offering a word of thanks. How badly she had misjudged him! How terribly her fear had warped and twisted everything!

Evan was lying on the couch when she crept into the house, and he held out an arm to her.

"Tessie! You're late. I tried to call you. How was it?"

Glad Tidings

"Awful!" Tears rose in her throat as she buried her face in his shoulder. "But I think—it would have been better—if I'd been willing to listen."

Day 15: Glad Tidings

"How are you feeling tonight, Tony?"

Ida Roberts slipped behind the flimsy curtain that provided the child's only relief from the bustle and noise of the ward and rested a hand against his flushed cheek.

"Still pains pretty bad, ma'am, but I'm gettin' used to it. This bed's sure a sight more comfortable than anywhere else I've slept."

He offered a brave smile, and Ida's heart clenched. Suppose for an instant that Dr. Foster hadn't happened upon the accident! Would Tony have had any chance at all? By his account, he could claim nothing in the world but a spot behind some crates in an alley and a tolerably busy street corner on which to sell the Herald, and both of those had to be fought and scrabbled for on a regular basis. But there was no use thinking of it; God *had* brought the doctor along, and now it was their job to mend him up as well as they could.

She reached out to smooth the tangle of dark curls away from his forehead, knowing the action served no real purpose, but unable to resist the impulse. Tony's eyes slid half closed in the grateful way he had when offered relief from even the slightest discomfort. The child was small for his age but still desperately young, and so hungry for what ought to have been a mother's or a sister's hand.

"You give new strength to the word 'patient,' Tony. Most people grumble far more and with far less cause, you know."

Glad Tidings

"Don't know as it's much credit to me, ma'am. Kickin' about it won't bring my leg back. If I thought it would—I might try it."

There was something pathetic in the half-humorous, half-shamefaced way that he made the admission, and Ida blinked hard for an instant before smiling down at him.

"If it would help at all, Tony, I certainly wouldn't object. I'd put on a set of ear mufflers and let you 'kick' away."

The slight twitch at the corner of his mouth thanked her, and she belatedly remembered the task that had brought her to his bedside.

"Are you hungry? The doctor says you may have a bit of Christmas dinner if you want it."

The look of longing in his eyes was almost immediately swept away by the wave of pallor that washed his face, giving her a far more accurate account of his pain than his doggedly cheerful words.

"Don't know as I could stomach much of it, ma'am. I wouldn't want to take it away from nobody who could."

"Could you stomach some broth, do you think? You need to take something if you're going to get well and strong again."

Tony gave a faint nod, and Ida hurried to the kitchen, returning with a bowl of rich broth and a tempting bit of turkey that she hoped she could coax him to try. The child ate obediently, took another dose of medicine without complaint, then sank deeper into the pillows, white and worn with suffering.

Ida made a quick tour of the ward, confirming that her other patients were well settled for the night, then returned to Tony's bedside, drawn by an impulse she only half understood. She found him with his hand resting on a little tin horn that peeked from under the bedclothes, and somehow the sight gave her more pain than pleasure.

The toys from the Christmas tree so graciously provided by a nearby Sunday school were all very well for poor children with a roof over their heads, but what good could they possibly be to Tony? She had a fleeting image of the little waif selling papers to the toot of a tin horn before remembering that his leg would likely prevent him from ever returning to that particular occupation. But if he could find any comfort in the impractical offering, she would be the last to rob him of it.

"Did you have a good Christmas, Tony?"

"Oh, yes, ma'am." His voice was soft with pain, and she reached to smooth his hair again. "'Specially those singers. My, weren't they fine?"

The carolers in question had certainly been enthusiastic, though their propensity to wander off key had left Ida's ears aching, but she smiled down at the boy.

"It was certainly kind of them to come and sing for us, wasn't it? Which song was your favorite?"

"The one about 'glad tidings.' I didn't quite take it all in. Do you know what they were singin' about, ma'am? It almost—well, it 'minded me a bit of a newspaper."

The way the makeshift choir had belted out "Shout the Glad Tidings" *had* sounded a bit like the raucous calls of a flock of newsboys, now that she thought of it, but Ida tried hard not to smile.

"I suppose you could say it was a bit like a newspaper, Tony. 'Glad tidings' means good news, you know. They were singing about the good news of Christmas."

"Is it good news, ma'am? I ain't touched a paper for days."

"Oh, well, this news wouldn't make the papers, I'm afraid." Ida sighed. "It's the news the angels brought to the world. 'Good tidings of great joy, which shall be to all people,' you know."

Tony's brow drew into a little, puzzled frown, and he sighed.

"Must've missed my corner, I guess. But it don't matter so much. Good news don't usually sell so well anyway. Do you know what it was, ma'am? I'd kinda like to hear it, for all that."

And Ida Roberts, who had given herself over to be the hands and feet of Christ without the slightest idea of ever being used as His mouthpiece, suddenly found herself face to face with a soul seeking light that her careful touch alone could never give. But as she looked into the rich, dark eyes of the boy who had softly stolen her heart, what could she do but tell him?

Day 16: Sign

Donnie Atwater stared at his textbook without really seeing it, his talk with his mother echoing through his mind.

"Dad and I can't tell you what you should choose, son. We trust you to pray about it, and we'll be proud of you either way. But Mr. Royce needs an answer by the end of the week."

Lord, what should I do? Pushing back from the table, he began pacing the length of his small room. *I was sure this was where You wanted me, but is it still? Is this a distraction, or is it Your leading?*

Mr. Royce's offer was a generous one: the salary was good, the prospects excellent, and he'd be able to live at home, with all its familiar connections. And while he enjoyed Bible college, it had never been the easy choice. Rooming with his aunt's family lowered his board costs, but four children under the age of ten made the house incredibly noisy, especially during study hours. Working his way left him time for only a few church activities, and he hadn't yet formed any deep friendships with his classmates. But the most important question remained—where was God calling him?

Lord, would you give me a sign, please?

He dropped onto his bed and opened his Bible, turning the pages slowly. A cough sounded from the doorway, and he looked up to find the oldest of his young cousins standing there.

"Angie, what are you doing up? Didn't your mom say you were supposed to stay in bed?"

Glad Tidings

"It's lonely in there. And I'm cold." She shivered, and Donnie let his Bible fall back onto the bed and stood up, taking her gently but firmly by the arm.

"All the more reason you should be tucked up under your blankets and not wandering the house in bare feet." He guided her back to bed and pulled the quilts over her, then felt her forehead. He was no expert, but if Aunt Esther had been right in calling it only a slight fever, then it certainly seemed to have grown. Her cough was worsening too. Donnie brought her a glass of water, and Angela leaned against his shoulder as she sipped it slowly. When she had finished, he laid her back down, and she gave a little moan.

"Do you have to go?"

Donnie glanced at the clock and winced. He had hoped to use this rare quiet hour to study for tomorrow's exam, not to mention making a decision about Mr. Royce's offer, but he couldn't just leave Angela sick and alone.

"Want me to read to you for a little bit?"

"Really?" A hopeful spark lit Angela's eyes, and Donnie retrieved his Bible and sat down next to her bed, hunting up all the old favorite stories that he had loved as a boy. Angela's head moved restlessly, but when he paused for a moment, she turned wistful eyes on him.

"Donnie?"

"Yeah?"

"Do you believe it's all real?"

"Sure I do."

"Miss Sattler says so, but Daddy says it's just fairy tales."

Donnie's heart sank. He knew Uncle Stuart and Aunt Esther weren't believers, but he'd counted it as a hopeful sign that his aunt allowed him to take the kids to Sunday school, and he'd never considered that his uncle might be tearing down the good they were getting there.

"God's not a fairy tale, Angie. He's as real as you and me. More real, maybe, because without Him, we wouldn't even be here at all."

"I kinda hoped He was. I like hearing about Him."

Swiftly changing his focus, Donnie flipped to the gospel of John and began reading the beautiful promises of God's love and salvation. Angela seemed to be listening, but a heavy bout of coughing warned him that this wasn't the time for a discussion. Instead, he sought out more verses of love, protection, and comfort, silently praying that God would grant rest to his cousin in both body and spirit.

"I wish you didn't have to go home, Donnie." Angela's voice broke into a short pause, and she somehow sounded even more forlorn than when she'd been shivering in his doorway.

"I'm sorry, Angie. But you wouldn't want to be away from your home on Christmas, would you?"

Angela shook her head, and Donnie opened his mouth to say he'd only be gone for a few weeks but stopped at the sudden memory that he couldn't yet make that promise.

"Mom won't let us go to Sunday school with anyone but you, and I start feeling all mixed up again when I can't ask Miss Sattler things."

Donnie's heart squeezed. He had only talked to Linda Sattler a few times, but her love for the girls in her class had instantly earned his respect. She was just the person to work with Angela, but could he somehow help her gain his aunt's trust? And did he still have the time?

Donnie absently thumbed the leaves of his Bible, until he found himself in the gospel of Luke. Smiling at its appropriateness, he flipped back a few chapters and began reading the story of the first Christmas.

"And this shall be a sign unto you; Ye shall find the babe wrapped in swaddling clothes, lying in a manger."

The words hit him with unexpected force. Hadn't he asked for a sign? And hadn't God brought him a child, not wrapped in swaddling clothes or lying in a manger, but pointing the way clearly to work to be done for his Master? If God had called him here and given him influence over four rowdy, noisy little lambs that ought to be brought into the fold, could he just abandon them for the ease and security of home?

Glad Tidings

Is this my answer, Lord? Quiet peace crept into his soul, and he smiled down at his cousin, gently squeezing her shoulder.

"Don't worry, Angie. You'll have a great Christmas, and I'll be back before you know it."

Day 17: Praise

Samantha silently entered the gazebo and draped Josie's coat around her shivering shoulders. Her youngest sister clutched it close without lifting her head from the table as Samantha took a seat across from her. After a few minutes, Josie lifted her head but didn't look up—a sign that she was ready to listen, or at least to argue.

"Lee wasn't trying to make it harder, Josie. He's trying to keep Mom's memory alive for us, that's all. You know he misses her as much as the rest of us."

Josie didn't answer, but the absence of a rant against Leeland showed that she at least understood he was trying.

"You know Mom would want us to do this. 'Praise for a present' was her idea, remember? She never wanted us to forget our blessings, no matter how tough things got."

"I can't." Josie's tone was harsh, but Samantha caught the undercurrent of pain.

"I know it's hard, Jo. Believe me, I know. You—you were probably too young to understand, but—do you remember the year Mom started it?"

"We always did it."

"Not always. Well, probably always from your perspective, but—Mom started it the year we lost Dad. I know you don't remember him, but—you don't think that was hard? For her? For Lee and me, and Kelly and Jackson? This is—" Samantha nearly

Glad Tidings

choked on a lump in her throat as a rush of tears threatened. "This is the second time we've been through it, Josie. And it's tough. So tough. But Mom wanted us to remember—in the worst of times—that we could still be thankful. That we could still find reasons to praise."

"I. Can't." A hint of desperation laced her sister's voice. "You don't get it. I know—what Mom would want. But I can't, Sam. Not won't. Can't. There's not one single thing in the world I'm honestly thankful for right now."

"Oh, Jo…" Samantha slid from her bench onto the end of Josie's, slipping an arm around her sister. Josie's shoulders heaved with repressed emotion, and Samantha pulled her close. "Cry it out, Joey. I can take it."

Josie wrapped her arms around her sister's neck as hard, wrenching sobs wracked her body. Samantha didn't utter a word or offer a soothing motion that Josie would only have interpreted as a command to stop, just held her as the too-fresh grief washed over them in waves.

When Josie's sobs faded to gasping breaths, Samantha gently rubbed her back until she grew quiet, then sat her back and studied her red, tear-streaked cheeks.

"Goodness, girl, put that coat on right or Lee's gonna kill me!" She pulled the coat from where it lay across Josie's shoulders and helped her into it, zipping it snugly around her. Josie dug the heels of her palms into her eyes, then wrapped her arms around her chest. "Feel any better?"

"No." The word throbbed with pain, but it had lost its edge of defiance. "I'm never going to feel better again."

"Oh, Jo, I know the feeling. Trust me, I do." Samantha tried to meet her sister's eyes, but Josie looked away.

"When you guys lost Dad, you—you still had Mom. And you're all—all out on your own. You didn't need her like I do."

As much as the words stung, Samantha held her tongue. Her sister didn't mean to discount their grief; she was just too wrapped up in her own to see it. And Josie had always been Mom's baby, their bond knitting tighter as her older siblings left the nest. It was probably true that she felt the loss more sharply than anyone.

"We're here for you, Joey."

"I know!" The cry startled her with its violence. "And I'm supposed to have all this stuff to be thankful for, but I can't, Sam! I'm supposed to be glad I've got family and don't have to go into foster care or something, but it wouldn't matter if I still had Mom! And I'm supposed to be thankful that Lee and Alyssa moved back in so I don't have to change schools, but they wouldn't have had to if Mom was alive! And I'm supposed to be lucky Mom had that extra insurance to cover my college fund, but I don't want college—I just want Mom!" She doubled over as if in physical anguish, and Samantha closed her eyes and drew a deep breath.

No wonder Leeland had had such a hard time with Josie in the last few weeks. They wouldn't have been his words; probably some well-meaning church acquaintance or distant relative trying to paint a silver lining on a cloud that hadn't yet spent its rain.

"Listen to me, Jo." She drew her sister's head to her chest and held her close again. "Nobody here expects you to see the good in Mom being gone. Not for a long time. Maybe not ever. But that doesn't mean there's nothing left to be thankful for. You'd give up all the best parts of your life right now to have her back, I know. But Joey, would you give her up—everything she was and everything she meant to you—if it meant you didn't have this pain?"

Josie was still for three long breaths, then she shook her head slowly.

"Then praise God for that, Josie. Praise Him for all the wonderful memories He gave you. Praise Him for all the things you're going to miss most about her. Praise Him that it only hurts so bad because she loved you so much."

Josie drew a long, shaky breath like a trapped diver finally coming up for air.

"Lee would freak." A hint of a chuckle escaped her, and Samantha resisted the urge to pull her tighter and let her go instead.

"Maybe don't put it in quite those words. Lee's been through a lot too. But it would mean everything to him if you could find

Glad Tidings

something to be thankful for, Josie. Even if it's just a memory—for now."

Day 18: Wonder

"Dississ, Gampa?"

Emma held another ornament up to my face, and I took it from her hand to study it.

"This is from your—" What ridiculous names had they chosen again? "—your Mimi and Popi's wedding."

"Iss pitty!" Emma exclaimed, the same way she had for a plain red ball and a chipped rocking horse. She took the set of bells and ran with it back to the tree, stretching to place it as high in the lower branches as her arms could reach.

"Ugh, Mom!" Andrew looked up from the box of ornaments in disgust as his sister bent to give her daughter another. "Why do you even still have this old thing? I'm throwing it away this year!"

"Do it, and one of your presents goes with it!" Sue's voice called from the kitchen. Andrew wrinkled his nose.

"What if Jordan does it?"

"Then you both lose a present!"

"Dississ, Gampa?" Emma pushed another ornament into my hand.

"Just bury it in the box, and maybe she won't notice." Jordan spoke in a whisper, but Sue's ears were as sharp as ever.

"Don't you dare leave it in the box!"

"You don't even know which one I'm talking about!" Andrew threw his hands in the air.

"Doesn't matter! I want every single one of them on that tree."

67

Glad Tidings

Emma was still waiting, and I bent down and studied the ornament.

"This is—it looks like one your uncle Jordan made in third grade."

"Oh, not that one!" Jordan reached for it, and I handed it back to Emma before he could snatch it away. "Come on, Grandpa! At least let me hide it in the back somewhere. C'mere, Em; look, I'll trade you."

"Oooh, Emma, let me see!" Andrew bent over for a better look and burst out laughing. "Oh, bro, that haircut is golden! I want a picture." He pulled out his phone, and Jordan dove to block it, nearly knocking over his niece.

"Are you two ever going to grow up?" Michelle picked up her daughter and set her down on the opposite side of the tree from her brothers, who were now wrestling over Andrew's phone.

"Oh, just wait, Sheldon. There's got to be a good one of you in here." Andrew abandoned the phone to dig through the box again, and Michelle crossed her arms.

"One more 'Sheldon' out of you, and you'll wish you hadn't."

"You and what army?"

"Oh, I don't need an army. I'll just sic Emma on you the next time she needs a change."

"Oh, Shel, that's cold!" Jordan burst into laughter as Andrew's eyes went wide with horror.

Michelle was right about one thing; none of them seemed to have changed much from the time they were small. Sue's house for as long as I could remember had been boisterous, noisy, and full of life, the very reason I wasn't going to saddle her with a jaded, decrepit old man.

Making the trip this early had been a mistake; Sue had gone and moved Andrew's things into the basement and was talking like she wanted me to stay for good instead of the month. But I had never fit the busy, carefree life that I'd always wanted her to have, and I fully intended to find myself a corner in a rest home as soon as Christmas was over.

"Dississ, Gampa?" Emma held something up in front of my eyes, and when my hand closed around it, my body went cold. Blood. So much blood. Screams. A chopper. Too much gunfire. I opened my hand and looked down at the small object.

"Sue?" The word wavered, but the living room had gone quiet. What must I have looked like in that instant? Coming here had been a mistake. I was ruining their Christmas—

"Dad?" Sue's voice was worried as she knelt next to my chair. I could hear Michelle whispering something to Emma.

"Where—did you get this?"

Sue's eyes flew to the shell casing lying in my palm, and her face paled a little.

"Oh, Dad, I'm sorry. I didn't think. I always put it away—when you and Mom came, but—"

"Where, Susan?"

"Mom gave it to me. When I was a little girl. Brian had it etched and made into an ornament our first Christmas together."

She rolled it the tiniest bit so I could see the words "CPL Charles Scott, Vietnam, 1972" printed neatly on the brass.

"Why would you want—an old thing like that?"

Sue looked into my eyes, and her hand moved to grip over top of mine, holding the casing between us.

"Because this bullet helped save the life of a man who means the world to me. I know you can't talk about the war, Daddy. That's why I've never asked. But I'm so proud of what you gave. For your country. For your family. And I'm so glad you made it home."

"That's my favorite ornament, Grandpa." Jordan's voice was quiet, but when I looked up, he came to attention and snapped a salute. I'd been scared to death and proud as anything when he chose ROTC and set his sights on the Engineers, but I'd never thought I had anything to do with his choice.

What did any of them see in a broken-down old man who hadn't escaped the nightmares after almost fifty years? I'd fought to keep this life for them, but who in their right minds would want me to be part of it? Sue let go of my hand, and I stared down at the casing again.

Glad Tidings

"Emma, this one came from the place where Great-grandpa was a soldier." Michelle spoke softly, and Andrew jumped to his feet.

"C'mere, Em; I'll hold you up so you can hang it right at the top."

Emma's soft little hand reached to take the casing from my wrinkled and scarred one, and she gave me her best baby smile, looking just like Sue had before I'd gone away.

"Iss pitty!"

Day 19: Star

"Just what I wanted for Christmas." Beads of sweat stood out against Trev Dalton's pale face, despite the chilly air. Layla shook her head as she sank onto a mostly buried tree stump next to him.

"You have any idea how much worse off you could be right now? If it had rolled any farther, or if Nick and I hadn't been here—"

"Great. Lecture. Second thing I wanted most." Trev squeezed his eyes shut, taking quick, panting breaths as another wave of pain must have hit him, but finally he relaxed just the tiniest bit. "Fine. Go ahead. I deserve it. Just—make sure to save some for my mom. She'll want a—piece of the action."

"Trev, what were you thinking?" Layla couldn't keep a slight quiver from her voice.

"Wasn't."

"Yeah, that's pretty obvious." She bit her lip as he gave another sharp groan. "I wish there was something I could do for you."

"Just—not leaving—helps."

Was he serious? There hadn't been a question in either her mind or Nick's that one of them had to stay with him. Though in a way, Nick had drawn the easy job; at least he could do something besides sit and feel helpless. But dark was falling fast, and the last thing any of them needed was to crash the second snowmobile.

Trev shivered in spite of his coat, the emergency blanket, and the tarp they'd managed to drag him onto. Layla wished she were confident enough to do something for his leg, but with help coming as soon as Nick reached the house, it was best not to touch it more than they had to. She bent to pull the flimsy-looking blanket tighter around his neck instead.

For a long while, only Trev's heavy breathing and occasional moans broke the silence. The canopy of stars began to spread above them, and Layla sent up a silent prayer of thanks that no new snow clouds obstructed the view.

"Makes you feel—pretty small, huh?"

Layla jerked her eyes down to see Trev staring up into the brightly-peppered expanse. A verse of Scripture prodded her mind, though she guessed Trev wouldn't recognize the quotation. She'd only ever seen him at church when he got bored enough to accept Nick's standing invitation.

"When I consider Your heavens, the work of Your fingers, the moon and the stars, which You have ordained, what is man that You are mindful of him, and the son of man that You visit him?"

"Something like that, I guess." Trev pressed his eyes shut and gritted his teeth, his face starkly white in the nearly full moonlight. "Makes you wonder if it's really worth it. If there's—even any point to trying to make your mark."

That was not what she'd been trying to say, but her mind flashed back to a discussion she'd overheard between him and Nick that summer. Trev's voice hadn't sounded hollow and hopeless then; he'd been almost bursting with starry-eyed plans for the future.

"Did you ever hear back on those scholarships?"

"Denied."

"All of them?"

"Got the last one yesterday."

"Trev—" Layla's body suddenly went cold, but not from the snow. "You wouldn't—try to hurt yourself or anything—on purpose, would you?"

"No." Trev sighed, his breath leaving a long, misty trail in the frozen air. "Nothing like that, Layla. I promise. I just get to feeling like—what's the point sometimes? Why not—"

"Do crazy stunts and take insane risks?" Layla finished when he didn't continue.

"Something like that. I mean, who am I to think I could ever really count for anything? Why not have some fun while it lasts?"

"You know you count for something to a lot of people. How do you think Nick and I would feel if you'd completely rolled your snowmobile out here without anyone to help? What about your mom? And just because you didn't get those scholarships doesn't mean you can't still do something important with your life."

Trev gave a dry laugh that held no hint of humor.

"My own dad didn't think I was worth sticking around for, Layla. Forgive me if I'm pretty sure the world can get along without me."

Nick had hinted that his friend still carried deep insecurities from his father's abandonment, but Layla had never seen it for herself. Was the whole cocky attitude just a facade to hide his pain? Layla dropped to her knees in the snow and reached under the emergency blanket to grip his arm tightly.

"You listen to me, Trev Dalton. Forget everything I just said. Well, don't, but—put it aside for a minute. Look up at those stars. Did your dad know every one of them by name?"

"What?"

"Did he?"

"He wasn't an astronomer or anything."

"Just answer the question."

"No."

"Exactly." Layla bent closer. "But God does. He knows the name of every star in the whole expanse of the universe, and He cares enough about you that He counts the number of hairs on your head. Like you said, we should be nothing. We would be nothing—nothing and hopeless—if God didn't care about us. But He does, Trev. He loves you. And that makes you worth everything."

"How can you be sure of that?" The words trembled on a fragile breath.

Glad Tidings

There were so many verses she could give him—would give him, or ask Nick to, sometime. But promises meant less to Trev than real, practical proof.

"We almost didn't come today. Nick's been studying nonstop for his physics exam, and I didn't feel like going alone. But Mom—Mom, the study-before-you-play queen who's never liked the snowmobiles from the time we moved here—said he needed to get out of the house and we should go with you. If that doesn't convince you that God was looking out for you, Trev, I don't know what will."

"I—I'll think about it." Trev's teeth chattered, and Layla pulled the blanket closer as the roar of rescue vehicles warmed the frigid night.

Day 20: Wise Men

Anyone who had glanced into Professor Van Dolen's office on this particular Christmas Eve would have had some warning of the current of his mood, and any upperclassman who had ever ventured to approach him on the subject of the holiday would have been able to give at least a broad understanding of the reason for his undeniable "grouch." But Albert Ellis, being a freshman with no particular reason for seeking out the counsel of the eminent historian, had received no such warning, and so it was that he found himself ill prepared to meet the torrent of invective poured upon his head for deigning to offer a polite "merry Christmas" as he passed in the hall with an armful of packages.

"I presume you count yourself a Christian, young man?" was the inauspicious beginning, and when Albert answered rather blankly that he did, the professor's face clouded further. "And how do you propose to justify your claim of Christmas as a sacred celebration when you seem intent on marring its sanctity by indulging in the pagan practices of gift-giving—a direct derivation from the Roman Saturnalia?"

"I—that is—" Albert stammered, but as the professor's litany was well-practiced and only nominally dependent on his listener's replies, this incoherent answer did not upset it in the least, and Albert was treated to such a lecture as left those students who sat under the great Professor Van Dolen feeling it no loss to surrender their rather sizeable tuition.

Glad Tidings

The professor traced minutely the practice of gift giving from ancient times to the present, placing special emphasis on any instance where the Christian tradition might have been said to absorb existing custom, then branched off into such a mix of yule logs and evergreen boughs, sprigs of mistletoe and bouts of drunken revelry that poor Albert, who was still attempting to link his armful of small packages to those European rulers who had demanded Christmas tributes from their poorest subjects, was left completely bewildered. The harangue drew to a close with a scathing indictment of the modern spirit of commerce, which had taken a scarcely respectable farce of a religious festival and revived it in an even viler form, leaving it no merit whatsoever except to allow a rabble of shopkeepers to turn a fine penny, and when this final and most crushing salvo had been delivered, the professor turned back to his listener with an air of challenge that had made many an aspiring historian or budding divine mumble an appropriate penitence and retreat in haste.

But Albert Ellis, whose mind was, on the whole, more bent toward chemistry and mathematics than history and philosophy, possessed at least two qualities which his predecessors had not: the one being a sweet and simple faith learned at the knee of a beloved maiden aunt, and the other an innate distrust of conclusions founded on high-flown words and elaborate conjectures rather than solid, provable fact. Let it be noted that in the lives of Albert and his Aunt Patience, the doctrines and precepts of the Lord Jesus Christ were immovably fixed as the latter.

Though suitably awed by the professor's eloquent tirade, certain facts remained firm in Albert's mind. First, that his conscience acquitted him of any wrongdoing in connection with the holiday observances he proposed; second, that his dear Aunt Patience could certainly have done no wrong in teaching him to love and keep Christmas for the Savior's sake; and third, that just because certain men might have made a mockery of this holiest of days, it did not follow that all men must have done so, let alone that he should do so by attempting to celebrate it at all.

Angie Thompson

Whatever response the learned professor had expected from this "green" young freshman, the quietly confident smile that spread across Albert Ellis's face had certainly formed no part of it.

"Well, sir," he began humbly, but without a shadow of his earlier confusion. He might have been momentarily dazed by the sudden attack from an unexpected quarter, but he had regained his footing now. "I don't know nearly as much about all that as you do, and I daresay I shouldn't like to keep Christmas the way some folks have done. But I know why I'm keeping it, sir, and Who I'm keeping it for, and I can't see as He objects to my showing a little kindness to my friends in honor of His birth," this as he looked down at the packages on which the force of the professor's ire seemed to have been spent, "even if some Romans did have the idea before. Seems to me He didn't object when far wiser men than me brought gifts to Him at the first, and since some of these are bound for the little tree down at Davis's mission chapel, that makes it a gift to Him, as it's given to the poor, you know.

"But I expect He'll be pleased with your Christmas too, Professor, so long as it's done unto Him. If it wouldn't violate your conscience about the Romans and all, I'd ask you to come down to the mission tonight and hear Davis's message, all about how the Lord Himself was our greatest gift. He can say it all much better than I can, of course. Well, goodbye, Professor, and merry Christmas anyway!"

And the young collegian passed on through the hall, leaving the venerable professor for once in his life utterly speechless. Him keep Christmas! And keep it unto the Lord, when no such consideration had ever before entered his mind! There is a vast difference, you may notice, between pointing out the foibles of others and resolving to live up to the standard against which so many fall short.

It is perhaps a mercy of Providence that young Davis, whose roommate had been one of the professor's early conquests, did not note the visitor who occupied the far corner of a back bench in his chapel that night!

Day 21: King

"Any easier today, old man?"

The mix of pleasure and regret that lit Ford Paxton's wan face banished any lingering disappointment from the corners of Ned's heart.

"I told Father he shouldn't have asked you. You'd have a much better time at the sledding party than stuck up here with me. And I'll be downstairs again in a day or so."

"Think I'd have any fun if I knew I could have seen you and hadn't?" Ned settled in an easy chair near the bed and stretched his legs comfortably. "Besides, it's no hardship to be tucked away by a warm register instead of tramping up and down snowy hills until I don't know if I'm hot or cold anymore."

Pax shook his head but made no further protest, and Ned leaned forward with his arms on his knees.

"I say, though, you do know how to keep Christmas here! I thought it'd be dull as anything when Mother wrote that I'd have to stay at school over the holidays, but Cunningham's kept things at such a pitch that even the shyest chap couldn't help but enjoy himself."

"Oh, I'm glad of that!" Pale as it was, his friend's face glowed with pleasure. "I helped Father plan all that years ago, thinking how it would feel to be away from home at Christmas, and it's kept up splendidly. Though, speaking of shy chaps—is anyone seeing to young Jeffers?"

Glad Tidings

"I gave Knutsen a hint that the little chap wanted cheering up—like you said you might, you know—and I pity young Hobart when he comes back if he has to listen to many eulogies like the one Jeffers gave me last night."

Pax laughed, but his thin shoulders straightened a little, as if a load had been lifted from them.

"Knutsen's good for little chaps like that, for all he does set them thinking he's the next best thing to Teddy Roosevelt. The stories get them over the homesickness, and they lose their shyness when they go to repeat them. Then when a few of them get going on Knutsen's brilliance, they tend to find kindred spirits in each other and wean off their hero after a while. But it's good for Knut too; he's apt to get a bit reckless, and having so many young chaps looking up to him sobers him some. I'd rather add a new car to his train than have some others pick it up."

"You beat everything, Pax." Ned shook his head with an admiring grin. "I've never seen anyone read a boy's character faster, and then know exactly what's got to be done to manage him."

To his surprise, Pax blinked and swallowed hard.

"Well, I can't do much but watch, you know." His gaze drifted toward the corner where his crutches sat before pulling resolutely back to Ned with an unusually forced smile. "A fine substitute for a sledding party this is, sitting and watching me mope. Shall we have a game?"

"Only if you're up for it." Ned tried not to let his concern appear too obvious. A blue fit from Pax often meant that his back was hurting him more than he wanted to admit, and Ned had no desire to add the burden of entertaining him to his friend's troubles.

"It can't hurt me, or Father wouldn't have let you come. Mind bringing the table around?"

Ned quickly located the little table that fitted neatly over the bed, then brought out the chess board. Pax was unusually silent as they played, and Ned kept his thoughts to himself and concentrated on the game. But either his skills had unexpectedly improved or Pax's concentration was suffering, and Ned found himself in the novel position of placing his friend's king in check before five minutes had passed.

Pax immediately reached for his king to remove the offending pawn but stopped short when he found that a knight barred his way. He countered with a bishop instead, then laid an arm across his forehead and closed his eyes.

"Most useless piece in the game."

The words were murmured almost too low to catch, but Ned took his hand from the knight he'd been considering and studied his friend with a frown.

"What is?"

"Forget it." Pax removed his arm and trained his eyes on the board again, but Ned caught his wrist.

"Pax." He waited until the other boy met his gaze. "Tell me."

"It's nothing. A silly fancy. I just—" He broke off as though unwilling to finish the thought, but Ned waited him out. After a moment, Pax sighed. "Why does the king have to be the weakest piece on the board? He ought to be able to do so much good, but instead he has to be guarded by all the rest. A king ought to charge into battle with his men, not lie at home and let others fight for him."

The fact that he had used "lie" instead of "sit" cleared Ned's mind of any doubt that the principal's son was thinking of more than the chess board. He gently laid a hand over his friend's.

"You're looking at it all the wrong way, Ford." The other boy's head came up at the rare use of his given name, and Ned smiled softly. "Maybe he can't do as much as some, but do you think any one of them would give him up? Why, he's the one who draws them together and gives them a reason to fight at all. They'd be nothing without him, and they all know it."

Pax threw his free arm over his eyes, and Ned gave his hand a gentle squeeze and let it go.

"You're tired tonight, old man. Shall I go and let you sleep?"

"No, don't, please." Pax rubbed his sleeve across his face and turned back to the board with eyes that shone wet in the lamplight. "I think this useless old king might just pull through this fix yet."

Day 22: Ponder

"What you thinking about?" Blake's breath tickled my ear as he bent to wrap his arms around me where I stood gazing out the window.

"Mostly the message tonight, I guess."

"And Jade?"

I nodded slowly.

"I know it won't always be easy, but I'm so glad we made this choice, Blake. If anything, the message tonight just confirmed it. Maybe we can't help all the kids in the world, but even if it's just this one, it's so worth it."

"I agree." Blake kissed my cheek and my ear, then straightened and let me go. "And since we've got about a million packages to wrap before tomorrow, why don't you go make sure she's tucked away for the night and then come wrangle the tape for me?"

I stood on tiptoe to plant a kiss on his cheek, then quietly ascended the stairs. Jade's door stood ajar, and I peeked in to find our little foster daughter in her pajamas, curled up on the end of her bench in the embrace of the oversized teddy bear that had been Blake's welcome present. At the pensive look on her face, I swallowed my question about what she was still doing up and slid onto the other end of the bench.

"Anything you want to talk about tonight, Jade?"

Beautiful dark eyes peered up at me from a face the shade of creamy milk chocolate, much too mature and wary for her eight

Glad Tidings

years. I wanted to gather her up and hold her tight, thanking God that she was finally somewhere safe, but I knew she had to make the first move.

"I was just thinking." She scooted a little farther into her bear, her eyes dropping with the old reticence she'd shown during her first weeks in our house, especially when it came to asking for anything. I had thought we were past all that, but the social workers had warned that certain issues would crop up in unexpected places, even after they seemed to be gone.

"Thinking about Christmas tomorrow?"

"A little." A smile teased the corner of her mouth, but then she grew serious again, pulling the bear's arm tighter around her chest. "And about—what that man said tonight."

Of course. How many awful memories had the guest speaker's message about the baby in the manger and the children living in poverty in our own community brought back? Again, I longed to reach out to her, but I held my arms still.

"Jade, you know I'm here to talk any time, okay? About anything."

Jade nodded slowly, running her lips across her teeth in a way that still signaled deep uncertainty.

"Anything you want to say, I won't be angry with you. I promise."

Her gaze darted up to my face, fell back to her knees, then slowly lifted again.

"Am I—getting Christmas presents?"

"Of course you are, sweetheart!" My heart wanted to weep, but I forced myself to swallow the lump in my throat. "Just wait and see what's under the tree for you tomorrow."

She took a deep breath, but her hands trembled as she pulled the bear's arm tighter again.

"Was there something special you wanted?" Her Christmas list had been pitifully tiny, so I'd had to improvise heavily, but if there was something she'd held back, I'd find a way to get it for her, even if it meant digging into my own gift money from Mom and Dad.

Jade mumbled something into the furry arm, retreating further into her soft fortress, and I leaned down.

"I can't hear you, sweetheart. Can you say it again?"

"I-wanna-give-my-presents-to-the-kids-who-don't-have-any."

"To the—" Her meaning slammed into me like a waterfall, taking my breath away. "Oh, Jade, sweetie, you don't—" Something stopped my tongue, and in the next instant, I remembered how I had felt as a child when my ideas were brushed off. "You want to give your presents—to the kids we heard about tonight?"

Jade lifted her eyes very slowly and scanned my face for a long moment before she nodded.

"Why do you want to do that?"

"Because I—" Jade licked her lips and swallowed hard. "Because I have so much stuff now. And they don't have anything. And he said—think about how much we have—and I did."

"Do you—want to give away your own presents? Or would you like to go to the store and get some other things to give them?"

"I want to give them mine." Jade looked down and fiddled with the bear's arm again. "I never had—something to give before."

For a long moment, all I could do was stare. Blake and I had been so excited for the chance to shower love on this one neglected child that it had never crossed our minds that she might see herself as one of the fortunate ones. And when had we thought of denying ourselves even a single gift in order to bless a stranger?

My thoughts flew to the electric skillet I was sure Blake had bought me. I could certainly make do with a pan on the stovetop a little longer—or perhaps give up the pair of boots I'd been eyeing and put that money toward a model with fewer bells and whistles. And if I knew Blake half as well as I thought, the new books sitting under the tree wouldn't stop him from joining in on whatever "his girls" chose to do.

"Let me—" I had to swallow hard again. "Let me talk to Blake, okay? We'll find out what time that mission opens and see when we can go down there."

Jade dove away from her bear so fast that it flopped onto the floor, and before I knew what was happening, she had wrapped her

Glad Tidings

arms around my middle and was hugging me tight. Tears filled my eyes as I gathered her up and held her close, and her whisper breathed warm in my ear.

"I love this Christmas!"

Day 23: Jerusalem

"Can't I come to Jerusalem, Judy? Won't you let me see it again?"

Lexi threw a panicked glance at her mother as her grandmother's fingers tightened painfully around her wrist, and Mom laid a gentle hand on Grandma's wasted arm.

"Soon, Helen. Very soon. You need to rest before you go out, you know. Close your eyes for a bit."

"You won't let Judy go without me?"

"No, she'll wait. Don't worry."

Lexi bit her lip to keep it from trembling. She'd been through enough explanations of who she was and why she was visiting in the last few years that she'd thought she was prepared for the worst. But being mistaken for someone named Judy and talked to in fading but eager tones about Jerusalem and flat rocks and Marcia and Gail while Mom was apparently accepted as Grandma's own mother was far beyond the bounds of anything she had imagined.

"You won't go without me, Judy? I want to see it one more time before I go home."

"I—I won't." Lexi croaked the words, only slightly comforted by her mother's nod. But the weak promise seemed to reassure her grandmother, who closed her eyes and appeared to doze again, letting her grip on Lexi's hand relax. Mom drew her back from the bedside, pulling her close.

Glad Tidings

"I'm sorry, sweetheart." The words were a bare whisper in her ear. "I knew it was bad, but I didn't realize she'd latch onto you that way."

Lexi shook her head, too overcome to say anything. Aunt Irene hurried back into the room with a styrofoam cup of what was probably tea, and her tired eyes narrowed as she looked at Lexi.

"What happened?" She barely mouthed the words, and Mom sighed.

"I always said those old pictures of Judy looked a little like Lex." She tightened her grip as Lexi began to shiver, and Aunt Irene shook her head and nodded toward the door. "Sure?"

"I'll call you."

Mom didn't argue further, just drew Lexi out into the corridor and down to a vinyl-covered couch. Lexi buried her face in her hands as the tight knot of fear gave way to tears of grief, fright, and shame.

"I'm sorry. I thought—I could—"

"It's okay, sweetheart." Mom rubbed her shoulder gently. "It's hard to see her this way. And if I'd known she'd grab you like that, I would have warned you."

"Did you—understand anything she was saying?"

Mom drew a long breath and rested back against the couch, gently pulling Lexi with her.

"She's gone back to the years she spent with Aunt Ethel in Canada when Grandma Clay got so sick. Judy was Aunt Ethel's daughter, remember? You've seen pictures of them together."

She had vague recollections of two teenage girls in vintage dresses sitting on the hood of an ancient car but couldn't remember if one of them had been Judy. But somehow just knowing there was something real and tangible to Grandma's rambling helped a little.

"Why was she talking about rocks?"

"Flat Rock was the town." Mom smiled and nodded encouragement as Lexi's breathing began to steady. "Marcia and Gail were sisters who lived on the nearest farm. They made quite a foursome, from what I've heard. Did almost everything together."

"Then what about Jerusalem?"

"Jerusalem—" To her surprise, Mom's voice faltered, and she put a hand up to wipe at her eyes. Lexi laid a hand on her arm.

"It's okay. You don't have to."

Mom shook her head.

"No. There's a reason—I told her she could go. Maybe—a reason she thought of it." She swallowed hard and lifted her gaze to the ceiling. "There was a lady in Flat Rock who took a liking to the girls and sometimes had them over for tea and cake. When it came near Christmas, she decked the whole house out in gold, despite the hard times. Mom used to describe those rooms to me. It was the most beautiful thing she'd ever seen. The girls had been reading Little Women, and Judy suggested they call the place 'Celestial City,' but Mom proposed 'Jerusalem' instead, and it stuck. They would go over there every chance they could get and then talk over the glories of the real new Jerusalem and how it would compare. I asked her once why she never did things up that way in our house, and she only smiled and shook her head and told me there was only one true Jerusalem, and only one place on earth that would ever come close."

The tears were streaming down Mom's face by the time she finished, and Lexi drew what felt like her first deep breath in hours.

"And now it's Christmas—and she's—" She couldn't finish the thought, but Mom nodded. Lexi felt tears sting her own eyes again, but this time they weren't tainted with fear.

A door closed in the hall, and Lexi looked up to see Aunt Irene approaching. Mom stood and hurried toward her.

"Is it time?"

"I don't know." Aunt Irene hesitated as she glanced toward Lexi. "She's asking for—" She broke off, and Lexi swallowed hard.

"For Judy?"

Aunt Irene nodded, and Mom looked down at Lexi, tears still swimming in her eyes.

"You don't have to do this, sweetheart. You can stay out here if you want. You've said your goodbyes."

Slowly, Lexi shook her head.

"If—if it helps her—I want to try."

Glad Tidings

Mom squeezed her hand, and Aunt Irene led them back into the room. A nurse was talking softly, trying to quiet Grandma's frightened moans. Lexi drew her fingers from Mom's and approached the bedside.

"Judy!" The relief that spread over Grandma's face eased the pain of her bony grip on Lexi's hand. "You didn't go without me, did you? You wouldn't leave me here?"

"No, Gra—Helen." Lexi couldn't stop her voice from cracking a little as Grandma's too-bright eyes met hers. "You haven't missed Jerusalem. You'll be there soon. And we'll all be there with you—someday."

Day 24: Adore

Quiet snow dusted the windows of the stately mansion as Vida Crane rocked in her chair by the nursery fire, smiling down at the rosy bundle in her lap. It might be every mother's prerogative to think her baby perfect, but Vida was quite sure she had more reason than most.

The door edged open on well-oiled hinges, and a dark shape limped into the room, but Vida hardly noticed until a sharp gasp, a stifled cry, and a heavy thump brought her head around to behold a squirming mass of faded calico struggling up from the rug.

"Why, what on earth—"

"I'm sorry, mum. I'm so sorry. I thought everyone was gone." The girl seemed to have unusual difficulty regaining her feet, and Vida clasped her baby a bit closer.

"I thought all the servants had gone to church."

"They did, mum. I thought—but that was foolish. Of course you wouldn't leave Baby alone. I'm sorry I disturbed you."

"Wait." Vida put out a hand as the girl turned awkwardly toward the door. "You came to look after the baby because you thought we'd left him behind?"

"Yes, mum. I'm sorry. I should have known—"

"Don't be sorry. Come here a moment."

The girl advanced with a halting, uneven step, and Vida surveyed her carefully. Her hair and dress bore the marks of a long day of hard work, but her hands and face appeared freshly scrubbed and her apron newly changed.

"What's your name?"

"Jessie, mum." The girl kept her head bowed, but the mother's eye didn't miss the look of mingled longing and rapture when her gaze fell on the baby. "But you needn't bother to remember. I expect I won't be staying long."

This, then, was the new scullery girl that the housekeeper had complained of to her mother-in-law just this morning, declaring that she would never take on such a charity case again.

"Have you ever held the baby, Jessie?"

"Oh, no, mum!" The girl held out her hands in a frightened gesture. "I wouldn't! I've only cleaned the grates and scrubbed the floors a bit. And—well—once, the nurse asked me to—to stop with him a moment while she fetched something, but I didn't touch him, mum, truly I didn't!"

If Vida had harbored any doubts about her impulsive plan, the knowledge that William's old, clear-eyed nurse had trusted the girl to watch the baby a moment in her absence dispelled them all. She rose from the chair and nodded toward it invitingly.

"Would you like to hold him a moment?"

"Oh, mum, I couldn't!" Awe and fright mingled in Jessie's voice, and Vida smiled.

"Of course you could. You've given up your Christmas Eve to see that he was cared for. Why shouldn't you have some reward for that?"

"But he didn't need it, mum. I ought to have known—"

"You had a good and generous thought, and someone ought to have told you that I was staying home with the baby. But I'd like to thank you for looking after him the best you knew how. Come, sit."

The girl's halting stride was slower than ever, but she settled herself carefully in the chair, and Vida placed the precious bundle in her lap. Jessie's arms cradled it firmly, protectively, but not tightly enough to wake or frighten the little angel who slumbered there. Vida watched for a moment with a motherly anxiety that defied all her reasoned arguments, then she resolutely turned her back and strode to the end of the room, making herself minutely examine the exquisite madonna on the wall before returning to the pair in the rocking chair. When she reached them, tears were streaming down Jessie's thin cheeks, and she had turned her head away to keep them from dripping onto the baby.

"Why, dear, what is it?" Vida knelt next to the chair, and the girl raised a shining face to hers.

"I'm sorry, mum. It's only—this Christmas. So beautiful. I'll never forget it—wherever I go."

The baby stirred a little, nestled deeper into the crook of Jessie's arm, and dropped back into slumber, and Vida sat watching him for a long moment before she spoke again.

"What's wrong with your foot, Jessie?"

"Clubbed, mum. Born that way."

"And you were put out to service in spite of it?"

The girl swallowed hard.

"My folks are dead, and I won't beg. Maybe it'll be the workhouse in the end, but not because I didn't try."

"Does the work hurt you?"

"Not as much as I hurt it, likely. I do my best, truly I do, but I never did much but sewing before Pa died, and I suppose I'm not used to it yet. My hands get cold and numb, and then I drop cups and slosh water and leave spots; or the bucket bumps my leg and trips me; or I can't do things fast and right at the same time. And then sometimes I can't sleep for aching, and Cook has to wake me when I ought to be up already. But oh, mum, don't tell, please! I know I'll be used to it soon, if I only have a little more time."

Tears swam in Vida's eyes before the girl had finished, and a fierce determination rose in her heart. Nurse had spoken only yesterday of wanting help with light chores and needlework, and any girl set under her would earn her keep and be looked well after in the process. Her mother-in-law would balk at the added expense, but surely she and William could keep a girl of their own to look after the baby's things. William would laugh when she told the story, but Jessie's evident love for their baby would be sure to touch the tender place in his heart.

Glad Tidings

"Have you hung your stocking, Jessie?"

"Why, no, mum. I gave that up years ago."

"Hang it tonight, dear. I wouldn't wonder if there was something the baby wanted to give you."

Day 25: Gifts

A lump tightened in Blanche Channing's throat as the final notes of the old carol left her lips. Comfort and joy! The words seemed almost monstrous tossed into this sea of suffering soldiers—the ones who had marched away bravely for their country and come back marred for life. She'd heard the terrible stories from Pearl—missing limbs, blinded eyes, scarred lungs, the vague but terrible specter of shell shock. If only she could do something to help them! She had even gone so far as to ask Pearl whether she ought to save for a nurse's training course and been laughed at for her pains.

"You, kiddie! Why you'd faint dead away the first time you changed a bandage. No, don't look so glum; there's plenty else you can do, and where'd you get the money for the course anyway? Best run now; those fat little fingers won't train themselves, and we've got to have the rent next week, you know."

Pearl had been right, of course, both about her courage and the money, though the tin-sounding hospital piano that Blanche had finally worked up the nerve to ask if she might play on hardly counted as "doing something." How she wished she could give something real—even something as small as a pencil—to honor the men's brave sacrifice. But the influenza had played havoc with her students' lessons and her tiny savings, and she couldn't have scraped together enough pennies just now to buy ten pencils, let alone hundreds.

Glad Tidings

Blanche reached for the next page of her music, and the notes swam before her eyes. She blinked hard to clear them, but the little black dots that made up her bread and occasional butter continued to waver in and out of focus, and as she bent closer, a yawn caught her unaware.

"That's all for tonight, gents!" Pearl's commanding voice spun her around to see the tall redhead addressing the assembled soldiers. "You're all up after hours as it is, and no cranberry sauce tomorrow for anyone not in quarters in ten minutes flat."

Amid vague rumblings of mutiny and mutterings about "Sergeant O'Rourke," the group began to disperse, and Pearl hurried over to Blanche.

"Wait half an hour for my shift to end, and I'll walk you home, kiddie. It's no time for you to be on the streets alone." She bustled into another room, and Blanche began gathering up her music sheets.

"Miss?" The quiet word from just behind her startled Blanche out of all rational proportion, and her music cascaded to the floor as her cheeks flooded with heat. The soldier who had addressed her dropped to his knees to pick it up, and Blanche tried desperately to wave him away.

"Oh, don't! It's my own fault. Please don't."

The young man ignored her, continuing to gather the papers, and Blanche knelt next to him to help. When the music was stacked in her arms again, she slid it carefully into her portfolio, then turned back to the soldier, who still sat in his old position on the floor.

"I'm so sorry! Thank you. It wasn't—you needn't have—"

He shook his head with a smile that twisted into a grimace, and Blanche noted for the first time the crutch lying by his side.

"Oh, you haven't hurt yourself, have you? Can't you stand? Can I help you? Pearl!" This as a frantic glance around the room showed her friend emerging from a doorway. The nurse was beside them in two swift strides, surveying the young man with her hands on her hips.

"Captain Hartley, I'm thinking of beginning a catalog of what *can't* be done on crutches with you as my prime illustration. What were you thinking of this time?"

"I dropped my music. He was trying to help." Blanche twisted her hands together, and Pearl rolled her eyes.

"Of course he was." She picked up the crutch, then braced the young man with her strong arms as he rose to his one remaining foot. Droplets of sweat glistened on his forehead by the time he finished, and Pearl motioned to another doorway. "Come, Captain, back to bed with you. You don't want to miss the cranberry sauce."

"Loathe the stuff." He spoke through gritted teeth, but the attempt at humor reassured Blanche a little as she followed them anxiously to one of the wards and watched Pearl deftly check the captain's bandages and tuck him into bed.

"Stay a moment, kiddie, and keep him from tap dancing while I get something to help him sleep, will you?" Pearl threw a wink over her shoulder as she hurried away, and Blanche took a hesitant step closer.

"I'm so sorry. You shouldn't have—"

"Probably not, but I did, and it wasn't your fault. My fault for startling you to begin with." A touch of a smile crossed the captain's wan face. "And I don't think I ever did thank you, which is what I set out to do."

"Oh, please, you needn't. It's such a little thing. I wish there was something I could do—like Pearl and the girls—something real I could give, when you've all given so much."

"Miss—" The young man paused, and Blanche flushed.

"Channing. Blanche Channing."

"Miss Channing." He smiled. "You're a working girl, aren't you? Not flush with money, I expect. What do you do?"

"Give music lessons." Blanche swallowed hard, but the young man's eyes lit.

"Do you? Won't my mother be glad to hear that! She's wanted a new teacher for Nell for ages. And after a full day of listening to whining children pound out travesties on Bach and Handel, you

Glad Tidings

come here to play and sing for us until you're so tired you can't see straight?"

Blanche's eyes dropped to her shoes, and the captain took her hand.

"You have a gift, Miss Channing, one from God Himself, and you've shared it with us—everything you have. That's the best kind of gift, you know—the one that's your own."

Made in the USA
Columbia, SC
17 August 2022